# THE TREES
## AND OTHER STORIES

# THOMAS EMSON

Copyright © 2013, 2019 by Thomas Emson

All rights reserved.

No part of this publication may be reproduced, distributed, or transmitted in any form or by any means, including photocopying, recording, or other electronic or mechanical methods, without the prior written permission of the publisher, except as permitted by U.S. copyright law. For permission requests, contact [include publisher/author contact info].

The story, all names, characters, and incidents portrayed in this production are fictitious. No identification with actual persons (living or deceased), places, buildings, and products is intended or should be inferred.

Website: thomasemson.com

Twitter: @thomasemson

Instagram: @thomasemsonhorror

Book and cover design by Thomas Emson

Cover photo by Pavel Chagochkin from Shutterstock

Imprint: Independently published

# Contents

| | |
|---|---|
| The Trees | 1 |
| Border Country | 18 |
| In Sorrow Thou Shalt Bring Forth Children | 30 |
| When Soft Voices Die | 41 |
| Kings & Paupers | 51 |
| Sequence | 58 |
| The Jantot Hourglass | 70 |
| Where Moth And Rust Destroy | 77 |
| About The Author | 105 |
| Also by Thomas Emson | 106 |
| Acknowledgments | 107 |

# The Trees

The girl said, "They went in there, and they never came out."

"Never's a long time," said Police Constable Jasper.

The girl put her hands in her hair. Her eyes were wide and burning with fear. She said, "We called them on their cell phones, but got no answer. We yelled out their names, but they're not responding. They should've heard us."

"It's dense in there, Miss. People have got lost in these woods over the years."

"And have these people ever been found?"

Jasper pushed his cap back and scratched his forehead. He stared into the dark, tangled mass of Cottam Wood and furrowed his brow.

The girl said, "Well? Were they found?"

He said, "Before my time, Miss. I've only been here a year, you see, and there's been no trouble. The odd one's gone missing over the past twenty years, they tell me, and although they might not've been found – well – they were mostly kids and didn't bother telling the authorities when they got out, you know."

Rage coloured her cheeks. She said, "You think we're kids? You think we're just stupid teenagers? My brother's twenty-six, officer. He's an attorney. And Shabelle – "

"Shabelle?"

" – is a realtor and –

"A realtor – ?"

" – she's twenty-eight. We're not kids, we're – " She faltered, putting a fist in her mouth to temper her tears.

Jasper's gaze moved across the wall of trees. Oaks, beech, pine, and elm forged together by nature into a bruise of thick, impenetrable darkness on the landscape.

Jasper's wife had made costumes for the local playhouse's production of Macbeth two months previously. He remembered the bit about Great Birnam wood coming to Dunsinane. The production used local children dressed in green and brown, their faces streaked with rustic-coloured make-up and twigs attached to their hair, to play the moving trees. They were a friendlier looking forest than Cottam Wood.

"Officer," said the girl, "will you be organizing a search party?"

He fanned his face with his cap. The sweat poured down the back of his neck and it stained his shirt. "Best wait until morning," he said.

"Morning?" – her voice was a squeal – "Morning? They could be dead by morning. It's my brother and my sister-in-law," and she started to cry, her body shaking.

Jasper flushed. "Please – please, Miss. We'll – we'll find them, I promise – we'll – " and he reached out a hand to touch her shoulder, but she recoiled from him and stumbled away up the slope to where Jasper's patrol car was parked. The girl's boyfriend loitered near the car. He stared out across the patchwork of fields dotted with sheep and lambs. The sun beat down and the heat made things shimmer. Jasper shielded his eyes with his hand and watched the girl gesticulate to her boyfriend. She waved her arms around and whipped her head from side to side. They were Americans. Four of them: the girl, Jenny Gilligan; her brother, Larry and his wife, Shabelle; and Jenny's grungy boyfriend, PJ

Prying details out of them when he'd arrived at Cottam Wood after the 999 call, Jasper had said, "What's your full name, sir?"

"PJ, man."

"PJ Mann?"

"No, man, PJ, PJ"

"What does PJ stand for, sir?"

Jenny had said, "Paul Jeremy Turlow, it stands for Paul Jeremy Turlow, for Christ's sake."

"No way, man," said Paul Jeremy Turlow, "that's my slave name."

Now, Jasper tried to hear what Jenny was saying to PJ, but the couple was too far away. Jasper sighed and looked again towards Cottam Wood. A shiver fingered his spine. He glared into the gloom where the trunks and branches knotted into each other. They said that the deeper you went into the trees, the denser it got. And it was so clogged in places that a snake couldn't slither through. They said creatures that men had never seen crawled around in the heart of Cottam Wood. They said a lost tribe used the bones of those who'd gone missing in the woodland to build a city.

Jasper shuddered.

They said a lot of things, whoever "they" were. But only one thing was true: people had walked into Cottam Wood, and they'd not walked out. But that was more than twenty years ago.

The Friends of Cottam Wood, protectors of the area since the owner died twenty years previously, had fenced off the forest and posted

Trespassers will be prosecuted signs around the perimeter. But the signs failed to hinder Larry and Shabelle Gilligan.

An engine rumbled in the distance. Jasper glanced over his shoulder. Jenny and PJ still argued near the police car. A battered Volvo estate trundled over the hill and stopped next to Jasper's vehicle. Peter Hawtrey, chairman of the Friends of Cottam Wood, got out of the Volvo. He glanced over at Jenny and PJ and then limped towards Jasper.

Leaning on his walking stick, Hawtrey said, "You're having trouble with strangers, PC Jasper?"

Jasper nodded. "Two of them missing. They've been in there" – he threw a thumb over his shoulder in the direction of Cottam Wood – "for four hours."

Hawtrey's jaw tightened. "It has been a while since we had missing persons. Twenty years and more. We don't want any fuss, PC Jasper."

The policeman frowned. "No, we don't, Mr Hawtrey."

"I mean – what I mean is, Cottam Wood has a reputation – it's a protected site." Hawtrey made his mouth into a smile but there was no warmth in his eyes.

Jenny came back from the car with PJ and said, "We're going in to look for them."

Jasper shook his head. "Miss Gilligan, I can't let you do that. Cottam Wood is private property. You can't go wandering in there. Your brother and his wife shouldn't have done so, either."

She cocked her head to the side and folded her arms. "Well, help me look for them and you can arrest them, officer."

She started for the tree line. Jasper stepped in front of her, holding out his arms. "I can't let you go in there, Miss Gilligan."

Jenny glowered at Jasper. And then she said, "Do you realize who we are?"

Jasper sighed. "It doesn't matter who you are, Miss Gilligan, I don't have the authority to allow you to enter Cottam Wood."

Anger flared in her face. "Well who the hell has?"

Jasper watched the fury drain out of her cheeks, and then said, "We need permission from the Friends of Cottam Wood." He gave Hawtrey a nod and Hawtrey gave him another cold smile.

The girl glared at the trees. "That place doesn't deserve friends," she said, "it deserves to be burned down."

Cottam Wood rustled, a whisper bristling through its dark heart. Jasper felt something crawl up his spine and he trembled. "Mr Hawtrey," he said. "What do you say? Could we organize a search party?"

Hawtrey studied the trees. Jasper looked into the man's narrowed eyes. Hawtrey held his breath and remained focused on Cottam Wood for a few moments.

Jenny said, "Look, man – "

And Hawtrey, blowing air from his cheeks, said, "Naturally, PC Jasper – of course, they must be found." He raised an eyebrow, gazing at Jasper. "You'll go with them?"

"I shan't let them go, Mr Hawtrey. My suggestion would be to get some men ready for the morning from – "

"No."

Jasper and Hawtrey jerked.

"No," she said again.

Jasper said, "Miss Gilligan, please be – "

She stamped her foot and said, "My brother's lost in those goddamned woods. We're going with you, and we're going now."

"I can't let you do – "

"Officer," she said, striding towards him, "I want my brother and his wife back or I'm – " She tailed off and a spark lit in her eyes. "I've called my dad, okay?"

"Good," said Jasper, "I'm sure he'll tell you to leave this to us."

"My dad's the U.S. Ambassador."

Jasper put his hand to his forehead. "Really?"

"The U.S. Ambassador?" said Hawtrey.

"Yes, that's right," said the girl, "and he says, my dad says, he says he'll have you all – all of you – fired unless we find Larry and Shabelle before nightfall."

Jasper looked at Hawtrey and Hawtrey raised his eyebrows, saying, "You'd better go with them, PC Jasper. Just the three of you, eh. No need to alert anyone else, I shouldn't think."

Jasper said, "I just don't – " but Hawtrey interrupted him, saying, "I'll wait an hour, and if you're not back, I'll contact your police headquarters – and the U.S. Embassy, of course." He gave Jenny a sharp little bow.

Jasper shrugged and sighed. "Well, then . . . "

"Good," said Hawtrey.

"Come on," said Jenny, marching towards the trees.

Jasper said, "We should be all right, Mr Hawtrey. We have our mobile phones."

"Of course – of course you'll be all right."

Hawtrey smiled but again it didn't reach his eyes.

Twilight greyed the sky. Jasper looked up at the dying light and it chilled him. He bit his lip and watched Jenny and PJ walk towards the trees. He said to Hawtrey, "I'm two months from retirement – the last thing I need is the U.S. Ambassador on my case. Imagine me, after thirty years of duty, causing an international incident."

Hawtrey said, "I'm sure it'll die down once – once this is forgotten. We just don't want a fuss, that's all. Take care, PC Jasper – and mind your step in there."

Jasper told him goodbye and trotted off to join Jenny and PJ, and together they walked into Cottam Wood, and Cottam Wood engulfed them.

"Wow, that's weird," said PJ "It's like – like the light just died, man."

"And it's so hot in here," said Jenny. "And not nice hot, either."

"Sweltering," said Jasper. The air had thickened. Ten paces ahead lay darkness so deep, Jasper couldn't see beyond it.

PJ said, "Stinks like dead stuff in here, man."

Jasper sniffed. A hint of rot staled the air. The breath he drew in was too hot and putrid to feed his lungs. He cringed and put a hand to his chest. Sweat drizzled down his brow from under his cap.

Jasper glanced over his shoulder. Through the gnarled branches he saw Hawtrey. The man stared into the woods for a few moments. And then he took out his mobile phone and made a call. He nodded, his mouth moving as he spoke. But he was too far away for Jasper to hear his words. Hawtrey tucked the phone back into his pocket. He dipped his chin in a bow and seemed to mumble something. He raised his walking stick. Jasper raised his hand, thinking for a moment that Hawtrey was waving at him. But Hawtrey wheeled around and limped up the slope towards the cars.

Jasper stared out at the day that seemed to have no claim over Cottam Wood. The trees let no light in; not a drip of it penetrated the dense canopy. Jasper's legs twitched. His lungs craved clean air, and an impulse to leg it out here fired his nerves.

But Jenny said, "We've got to get moving or it'll be dark – and we'll never find our way out of here," and she went deeper into the trees.

PJ cast his eyes towards the canopy of branches that blotted out the sky. Jasper's gaze turned upwards and he stared at the ink-black covering.

"Come on," said Jenny, her voice distant.

A single track had been gouged into the earth and it snaked into the forest. Jasper traced it as far as his gloom-accustomed eyes could see, and then darkness devoured it.

He looked into the belly of Cottam Wood.

The trees pressed together, and branches swarmed from them and tangled with branches from other trees. Dampness coursed from the black and rotting bark of the trees and roots coiled from the earth at their feet.

Jasper glared at this and his vision became fuzzy.

And he saw things in the gloom.

He gasped, and his throat went dry. Knots of branches blurred into limbs: he saw arms and he saw legs, he saw heads and bodies. They were dark and shrivelled, the same colour and texture as the trees.

The strength drained out of him. He shook his head and blinked to clear his vision. And he saw that there were only branches.

He followed the path. Twigs scraped against him. Roots snarled his feet. His boots sunk into the moist earth.

And PJ said, "What the hell is that smell, man? It's like the whole place is, like, decaying or something."

"I'm sure it's nothing," said Jasper. He craned his neck to try and see Jenny up ahead. He quickened his pace and after two-dozen yards he saw her, pale and fragile against the gloom. He blew air out of his cheeks. He called her, and she stopped and turned around. She looked like a ghost and her eyes were filled with fear.

"All right," said Jasper, gathering them together on the path, "it's getting denser in here, now. We need to stick together."

"Maybe we should do like Hansel and Gretel did," said Jenny.

Jasper frowned at her.

"You know," she said, "leave a trail of bread or something. So we can, like, follow it out if we get lost. If – " She trailed off and her gaze swept around the darkness. "If we, you know, get to the witch's house and she wants to eat us."

Jasper's throat was dry, and he swallowed. But he didn't have any spit.

"Or string," said PJ "Tie a piece of string to a tree and follow it out. Like Theseus, man. Like Theseus did when he had to go into the labyrinth to kill the Minotaur."

Jasper curled his lip at PJ and PJ rolled his eyes.

"Greek myths, man," said PJ "Don't you have, like, school here?"

"We haven't got string," said Jasper.

"Or bread," said Jenny. She shrugged. "It'd be no good anyway – birds would eat the crumbs."

Jasper narrowed his eyes. He looked around. His eyes widened, and he lifted his gaze up to the canopy of branches that blacked out the sky.

"No birds," he said.

PJ and Jenny looked at him and PJ said, "Huh?"

Jasper said, "We've not heard a tweet since entering Cottam Wood."

"And no animals, either," said Jenny.

PJ, his gaze ranging the trees, said, "It's like life got lost here – or – or it never found this place."

Jasper looked back over his shoulder. Nothing but darkness. Goosepimples popped up all over his body. He said, "We'll be all right," and his insides churned.

They walked on. Jenny started to call for her brother and his wife.

"How big is this place?" said PJ after they'd walked for about twenty minutes.

"A good five acres," said Jasper.

"Jeez, man, that's crazy. Hey, Jenny, man, I hate it here. Let's go back."

"No way, PJ, not till we find them," she said. She called out again: "Larry! Shabelle! Larry!" And then she said, "They're in here, PJ, and we're not leaving without them."

She strode down the path, sweeping branches away with her arms, her feet churning through the mud.

Jasper bristled and said, "That's not up to you, is it, Miss Gilligan. I think Mr Turlow's right and we might start thinking about turning back. I didn't realize how dense it was in here."

Jasper scanned the surroundings. Sweat poured off his body. Heat made him dizzy. He called out to the girl, but she'd disappeared. Jasper's heart quickened. He could hear her shout for Larry and Shabelle, but the woods muffled her voice. Jasper turned to speak to PJ, but PJ had gone, too. He put his fingers to his temple and a pulse throbbed there. He called out – "Miss Gilligan, Mr Turlow . . . " – but got no response.

He hurried on. Something cracked under his foot. He gasped, raised his foot and looked down. He squatted and poked his finger into the mud. He touched something hard that didn't feel like a branch – the texture was all wrong. He creased his brow. He burrowed his fingers into the mud and wrapped them around the –

His insides chilled.

He yanked it out of the earth and held it up and saw the whiteness of it through the coating of mud.

Jasper leapt to his feet and staggered backwards, still holding the human bone.

He leaned against an oak and dampness oozed from the bark to paste his back to the tree. He stared at the bone. It looked like a tibia. Jasper panted, his head spinning. He threw the bone aside and stumbled down the path. He fell on his hands and knees and crawled along the path, clawing at the sludge with his fingers. His hands found bone again. He gashed out the earth and scooped out his find. He drew it up to his face and his mouth fell open. And when he stared into the skull's eye sockets, he felt his mind drizzle away.

A shriek tore through the darkness.

Jasper fumbled with the skull and then dropped it. He struggled to his feet. He groped through the trees, moving towards the noise. He snapped his mobile phone from the clip on his belt and stared at the screen.

The screen said No Signal.

Another cry, and Jasper quickened his pace. Things cracked under his feet as he dashed along the path and he hoped those things were branches. The path narrowed. The trees clawed at him. They tore his clothes and ripped his skin. He ignored the ache pulsing through his body.

He saw Jenny up ahead, kneeling on the path with her head in her hands. She screamed again.

Jasper shouted her name, but her eyes were fixed on something and she didn't turn around. He reached her and rested his hands on his knees. He panted, his heart racing. Jasper raised his head to look where Jenny looked.

And he stopped breathing. His heart seemed to swell in his chest. The blood left his face and for a moment he thought he would faint.

Larry Gilligan wasn't dead, but Jasper knew he could never survive – even if they untangled him from the snare of branches and got him to a hospital. Gilligan reminded Jasper of a puzzle: a figure trapped in a frame that you had to unravel.

Two boughs trapped his right leg, which had snapped mid-thigh. The bone jutted through skin and denim. His left leg slanted outwards at the knee. The angle was impossible, his foot caught up in vines and roots that were at waist level. His collarbone stabbed out of his upper chest, blood soaking his T-shirt. The right arm had been yanked back in a web of branches. Another branch forced his mouth open like a bridle. The bark broke his teeth and tore his gums. His cheeks were ripped almost to his ears as the bough pulled his jaw apart. Blood and saliva drizzled over his chin. His chest rose and fell rapidly as he wheezed for air. A stain spread over the crotch of his jeans. The man's eyes were wide and bloodshot. He shrieked against the gag in his mouth. Two stakes burrowed into the back of his head and sank deeper into his skull every time he tried to inch away from his bridle.

Jasper lunged towards Gilligan. "We've got to get him free, get him free," he said. He grabbed the branch pressing into the man's mouth. Leaves rustled and branches creaked. The man's eyes rolled back and he twitched. Jasper stepped away and stared.

"They grabbed hold of him. Did you see?" said Jenny. "Did you see when you tried to free him that they grabbed hold of him?" And then she cried, saying, "Larry, baby, oh, Larry."

Jasper took his penknife and hacked at the vines and twigs meshed around Larry Gilligan. They dropped away only to wind themselves around other parts of his body. Jasper felt breathless and hot. The trees seemed to have closed in on them. The air hung dense and putrid. He thought about the skull and the bone, and adrenalin flushed his heart.

PJ came screaming along the path saying he'd found Shabelle, but he stopped dead and shut up when he saw Gilligan.

But then he said, "She's like that, man – she's like Larry. All tied up. Her neck jammed between two branches. Her body all twisted and broken, man. Like she got stuck. She's dead. Shabelle's dead."

"Are you sure she's dead?" said Jasper.

"I know what dead is, man. She's not breathing. And she's blue, man – she's blue."

Jenny wailed. She punched numbers into her mobile phone. Jasper saw her and said to PJ, "You do the same. Get a signal. Dial 999 and ask for ambulance and police." And PJ, whimpering, got his phone out.

"There's no signal – there's no signal," said Jenny, her voice a high-pitched squeal. She hurled the phone and it smashed against a tree.

Jasper said, "Take me to Shabelle, PJ."

They raced back up the path, and then PJ turned right along another tree-lined corridor. "How many paths are there?" said Jasper.

"I don't know, man, how the hell do I know?"

This route was narrower. They had to stoop to make it through. The branches hung low. Jasper and PJ swiped them away from their faces as they darted through the darkness.

Then, before PJ said anything, Jasper saw Shabelle.

Her red dress provided a splash of colour against the gloom.

PJ said, "There, there," but Jasper was already moving towards her.

Shabelle Gilligan was dead. The boughs had ripped her dress and the earth had soiled her white shoes. Like her husband, she'd been tangled up in the branches. They'd coiled around her. A twig had poked her eye out and blood stained her face. Her torso faced the opposite direction to her lower body. Her legs were snared between two, chunky limbs.

"What are you going to do, man?" said PJ

"I don't know yet."

He turned, brushed past PJ, and strode up the path.

Jenny screamed from somewhere in the dark.

Pins and needles pricked Jasper's skin. He quickened his pace. He got lost for a moment, shot desperate glances around the gloom, and then found the path. He came around the corner to the place where they'd found Larry Gilligan, and he froze.

Jenny screamed again, this time staring at Jasper with her face twisted in terror.

"Oh, God," said Jasper, and hurried towards her.

She'd tried to free her brother and got her arms lodged between two branches. She'd tried to wrench herself free using her foot as leverage, but her foot had slipped and got trapped in a coil of twigs.

"Help me," she said, "help me, please."

The stink of methane saturating the air hung so heavy that Jasper could imagine it belching yellow from the carcasses that congested Cottam Wood.

He scurried forward to help Jenny.

He tried to yank her arms free. She screamed.

"I'm stuck, I'm stuck," she said.

"This is the heart of hell, man," said PJ behind Jasper.

"Help me get her out, PJ," he said, not turning around.

Jenny wailed and tugged. A knot of roots burst from the earth like entrails from a swollen corpse. Jenny's other foot got lost in the roots and they tangled around her calf.

She was almost doing the splits.

Her face lay on her brother's shoulder. Gilligan was almost dead – or already dead, Jasper hoped. Jasper stared at the suffering man for a few moments, but then he drew away his gaze.

Jenny's arms had slid further between the boughs. They were stuck fast up to the elbows. She screamed. A branch swayed. Her bones cracked. Her face blanched and she shrieked in short, sharp bursts. The branches pressed together. Jenny's arms twisted. She wailed and jerked and whipped her head from side to side.

Jasper stared at Jenny's arms breaking and he could do nothing to soothe her suffering. Bone spiked through the flesh of her forearm and her high-pitch shriek made Jasper shudder. Then, her eyes rolled back in her head and she fainted. Her leg snapped at the knee and she came to, making a terrible, guttural noise. Her mouth frothed, blood and saliva bubbling from her lips.

Jasper, tears streaming down his cheeks, said, "Don't worry, Miss Gilligan, don't worry. We'll – we'll get you out – phone your dad. He'll send people to help. He'll send the Army."

"Her dad?" said PJ

Jasper wheeled to face the youth.

PJ trembled, his face pale in the shadows.

Jasper said, "Yes, the U.S. Ambassador."

PJ gave a lunatic laugh and then said, "Her dad's not the U.S. Ambassador, man. She's always saying that to get free stuff, to get people to do things for her – to get cops to follow her to the heart of hell. He's – he's" – he started crying, shaking his head – "he's a concierge at the Ambassador Hotel in New York."

Jasper's mouth fell open and it wouldn't close. He turned back to Jenny.

The trees had her. They'd made a conundrum of her body.

"Go and get help, PJ," said Jasper, his voice a croak. "Just run – run and get help – run, and don't stop – just don't stop."

PJ got to his feet. "I don't know – "

"Just run."

And PJ ran, and Jasper heard his feet trample through the undergrowth, heard the crunch of leaves and branches and bones.

Jasper stared at Jenny and Larry. The brother was dead, his face grey and his eyes still. Jenny twitched now and again. Her eyes were shut. Froth boiled from her mouth. Jasper touched her arm. Her eyes snapped open and she screamed and thrashed about, and Jasper winced and took a step back from her as more bones cracked in her broken body.

She stiffened, her eyes wide and her mouth open. She seemed frozen, and Jasper stared at her. But then she let out a breath and sagged in the net of branches.

Jasper whined and went towards her, but his foot was stuck.

He looked down and sobbed. Roots curled around his ankle. His boot seemed to be wedged in the plants. He grew cold and tried to free his foot, but it stayed stuck. Jasper reached out a hand to steady himself. His palm pressed against coarse, damp bark, and the bark's soggy surface made his hand slip. His wrist lodged in a nest of branches. He whimpered and tugged, but the more he tugged, the more he got his arm jammed between the limbs.

A scream came from the forest.

PJ

He wasn't that far away, and he was saying, "Help me! Help me, I'm stuck!"

Jasper tried to free himself, but he got more tangled and he didn't want to move too much in case he suffered the same anguish as Jenny and Larry.

He stayed still, trapped in the branches. He listened to PJ's withering cries and he watched Jenny die.

The boughs caged him.

Apart from his trembling body, everything was still.

# Border Country

"I DON'T" – Crew punched his prisoner in the stomach – "exist, so whatever I do to you" – and he back-handed the guy across the face – "won't exist, either. The only things that'll be real will be" – he drove a boot into the man's chest, slamming him against the wall – "your wounds, your pain, and ultimately, your" – Crew grabbed the man by the throat, lifted him and the chair he was tied to off the floor, and headbutted him full in the face – "your death."

Crew dropped him back to the floor and stepped back to survey the damage he'd caused.

Blood masked the man's face. It bubbled from his broken nose, seeped from gashes above his eyes, oozed from his mouth. It soaked his shirt and drizzled from his body to pool on the flagstone floor. The man's chest heaved. He wheezed, every breath sounding like it hammered spikes into the guy's chest. A few of his ribs were cracked, for sure; and maybe one of his lungs had collapsed.

Crew, wiping the man's blood from his forehead with a handkerchief, said, "You're going to die, Sheehan. Here in this derelict cabin in the middle of nowhere. We'll bury what remains of you in the dirt. Your family may never find you. And if they do, there won't be much of you left. You'll be worm food. You'll rot out here and your soul will sink to Hell. Unless..."

Crew trailed off. He crossed to the window and looked out. He saw darkness, pitch-black emptiness. The cottage nestled in woods that lay a couple of miles north of the village. They'd grabbed Sheehan four hours ago and driven him up here. A helicopter team spotted the cabin a few days before, confirmed it as a good spot for Crew to work. Crew liked to do his stuff as near as he could to the prisoner's home; his family. That gave him a few extra psychological Billy clubs with which to beat his victim. He'd say something like, "Your little girl's down the road, scumbag. Should we go and get her and put her face on this red-hot ring instead of yours?"

Crew faced Sheehan and said, "I've got five guys out there, one of them top brass from London, and they're not going to go away until they know. That's bad enough. But worse still – for you, anyway – is that I'm not going to go away until they know. I'm going to ask you again, Sheehan, or I'm having another look in my briefcase."

Sheehan flinched. Merely hinting at the briefcase caused fear to flush through him. But he should fear it: that's where the hammer that broke his fingers came from; that's where the pliers that plucked out three of his teeth were kept; that's where the drill Crew would get next was stored.

"So tell me, Sheehan. What happened to the soldiers?"

Sheehan gurgled. Blood leaked from his mouth.

Crew stepped forward. "What's that you say, Paddy?"

Sheehan, tied to the chair with rope that was soaked in blood, flinched at Crew's approach. They all flinched at Crew's approach.

They flinched because he had no limits; no borders where his cruelty stopped, and you crossed into the country of compassion.

Crew leaned toward the man. He smelled piss and sweat and blood. He didn't care – they were common odours to Crew; this was how his job smelled.

"You will talk to me, Sheehan. You know why? Because I'm good at what I do, that's why. I don't hate you – not you, not your people. But that's why I'm so good, see. I have no hate. I'm a professional."

Crew straightened. He wiped his brow. It was clammy in the cottage. His shirt stuck to his body.

He said, "I've been in Northern Ireland ten years, Sheehan. Arrived in 1969 when the shit hit the fan, when you Catholics asked us Brits to protect you from rampant Protestants. And then what do you do, you IRA scum? Turn against us. Bite the hand that feeds."

He shook his head and scowled.

"So I know all about you and your weaknesses. You're back-stabbers and cowards, Paddy, that's what you are. And that's why you'll talk. That's why you'll tell me what happened to those soldiers before you die. You can't take it, Sheehan – you can't take what I can unleash. You've no idea what I am. I'm not a man. I'm an animal, pal. An animal. No compassion. No conscience. No regrets."

Crew crossed to the door and opened it. A breeze swept in, cooling his sweating skin.

He said, "You think about that," and stepped out into the night, shutting the door behind him.

He leaned against the cottage and lit a cigarette. He shut his eyes and let Sheehan and this mess slip from his mind. He thought about Carrie and the kids, and the wound of not seeing them smarted. He rubbed his chest where the hurt was centered. Six months since he'd seen them. A few phone calls to confirm he was alive, that's all.

Renfrew told him, "Do this job and you can go home; three months leave."

So here he was, doing this job.

He sucked on the cigarette and let Sheehan back into his head. Four soldiers disappeared here two weeks ago. This was IRA territory, bandit country, the badlands of Northern Ireland, and only a few miles from the border with the Irish Republic. It was no place for Brits. The troops, full of booze, had trekked out here to "kick the shit out of some Paddies" according to their mates at the barracks in Londonderry. But they never came back. And Crew got tasked with finding out what happened to them.

Do this job and you can go home.

He finished the cigarette and walked away from the cottage. The darkness was thick. He couldn't see a thing. But within a few dozen yards he started to make out shapes. Headlights flashed at him. The glare illuminated the cars and the figures milling around them. Crew threw them a lethargic wave.

"Have you voted today, Crew?"

"No, Mr Renfrew, I haven't. I've been busy."

Renfrew tutted. "You have a duty to vote, Crew. These freedoms we have, you can't take them for granted, you know."

"I never do."

"That's good to hear." Renfrew scowled, his bushy eyebrows meeting above his nose. "But do you know what they've done? Have you heard the news from London tonight?"

Crew shook his head. He scanned the group. Renfrew stood near the passenger door of the first black Rover. His driver sat behind the wheel. A pair of gorillas loitered at the back of the vehicle. Two other cars were parked up behind. Each contained four men. Plain clothed and narrow-eyed. Every one of them armed and ready to kill, thought Crew.

Renfrew said, "They voted for that woman. The greengrocer's daughter. We have a woman" – he said the word like it tasted sour in his mouth – "prime minister. Can you believe that?"

Crew believed it; the world was crazy.

Renfrew shrugged. "She's one of us, I suppose. And she's got some good men around her. At least we got rid of the bloody Socialists, eh?" He laughed and patted his belly. "Anyway. Politics is boring. Let's talk torture. How are we doing with the mayor of that ugly little dung-hole down the road?"

"He's tough."

"Is he? Looked a bit flabby to me – like I'm a good one to talk" – he slapped his belly again and chuckled – " but not really a hardened IRA man. He has no record, you know. No one here's got a record. They're clean. No Republican activity at all in that village."

"Maybe he doesn't know anything. Maybe no one does."

"You think?" said Renfrew, arching his eyebrows. "What happened to our boys then, Crew? UFO was it? Abducted by aliens?"

"They were looking for trouble. I'd say they found it. Pissed off farmer catches them on his land, blows them away. Maybe they crossed the border, found some girls and some Guinness."

"We still need to find out."

"That's more of a police matter; get the RUC over here."

Renfrew narrowed his eyes. "That sounded like an order to me, Mr Crew. Tell me it wasn't an order."

Crew sighed. "It wasn't an order."

"Homesick, are you? Missing the little 'uns? I've said: do this for us and you can take some leave; bed the wife; take the boys to the park."

Crew looked at Renfrew and wanted to stamp on his face.

Renfrew saw the look and said, "I don't care if you don't like me, Crew, I'm not here to be liked. None of us are. Just do the job you're paid handsomely by Her Majesty's Government to do."

"Give me the boy."

Renfrew, eyes fixed on Crew, raised an arm and clicked his fingers. Two men leaped out of one of the cars. They opened the boot and dragged out a youth. He whimpered and cowered as they hauled him over to where Renfrew and Crew stood.

"Here we are," said Renfrew, the boy thrown at his feet. "Don't get any of him on your shoes, Crew – these Paddies stink to high heaven; and they're hell to get out in the wash."

The kid looked sixteen or seventeen. His hands were cuffed behind his back. He trembled, his gaze flitting from Crew to Renfrew.

Crew stared at the lad and steeled himself, letting any beads of compassion ooze out of him. He grabbed the youth by the arm, said, "Come and say hello to your dad, sonny," and hauled him into the darkness, toward the cottage.

Crew shoved the door open and tossed the boy into the cottage. He went in after him, shut the door and said, "I've brought someone to see you, Shee – " and he turned around and Sheehan was gone.

The chair lay splintered on the floor. Pieces of clothes were scattered about, soaking up the mess on the flagstones. The ropes had been shredded. Blood dripped from their torn ends.

Crew stared at the sight. He felt his heartbeat speed up and a cold sweat broke on the back of his neck. He opened his mouth, but no words came out.

He held his breath and rushed into the kitchen. It was bare; just a sink gone black with age, the taps rusted. The back door had been torn off its hinges. Crew cursed loudly and ran back to the other room.

The boy kneeled on the floor. Crew strode over to him and the youth cowered. Crew grabbed him by the collar, dragged him to his feet.

"Where's your dad gone?" he said.

The lad, his eyes wide with terror, shook his head sharply.

How was he to know where his dad went, thought Crew; what a stupid thing to ask. But he was desperate; he was confused. He dropped the boy to the floor and turned to survey the scene.

And he noticed the bloody footprints.

"What the hell are they supposed to be?" he said, stepping forward.

It reminded him of those pictures of evolution you saw in textbooks: the ape lumbers across the page and slowly stands upright until the upright ape has changed into a man.

But these footprints went from man to –

He turned to the boy and said, "What are they?"

They led through to the kitchen. Why hadn't he noticed them before? Too frantic; too panicked. Calm down, Crew, he told himself, calm down; and he followed the footprints, entering the kitchen again.

Whatever made them went through that back door, and out into the woods.

A chill leached Crew's bones and he shuddered.

"Damn," he said, "this is a new experience."

It was: it had been a long, long time since he'd felt fear.

He walked back into the other room, following the footprints as they shrank back into the shape of a man's sole.

He looked at the boy and said, "What's going on here, son? Do you know what made these prints? Is this a joke, is it?"

The lad stared at him and said, "You think you're an animal?"

Crew furrowed his brow. He didn't have time for this. Sheehan had done a runner. Someone was playing tricks by painting those footprints on the floor.

"What's going on?" he said again.

The boy, pale, thin, glared up at Crew and something in his eyes made Crew's legs buckle. But he pulled himself together and grabbed the lad.

Screams tore at the night.

Crew froze.

The boy said, "They're here."

Crew went to the door and opened it. The cool night brushed his face and he shivered. The screams came from over where the cars were parked; where Renfrew waited for news of the missing soldiers.

"Come here," he said, grabbing the boy by the collar and dragging him out of the cottage. Crew took out his gun. He marched the boy toward the cars, holding him at arm's length, striding behind him, using the lad as a shield against whatever caused those screams.

"You're walking to your death," said the boy.

"Yeah? Well you're coming with me, then. And your dad, too, when I find him."

"You won't – "

Crew jerked the boy back, swung him round and pressed his face into the lad's face. Crew said, "I won't? Why won't I? What's happened?"

The screaming stopped. Crew heard growling. He looked toward the noise, narrowed his eyes against the darkness.

"Because," said the boy into his cheek, "he'll find you."

Crew pushed the youngster aside. He headed for the cars, gun held out ready to fire. Sweat poured down his back. He could smell it. I need a shower, he thought; get rid of this Irish stink.

He said, "Mr Renfrew? Mr Renfrew, are you there?"

Crew ducked down as he approached the cars. The windshield of Renfrew's car seemed to be blacked out. The driver's door and the passenger door were open.

Crew called out again, first to Renfrew, then the other men.

He came to the car and he straightened, holding his breath. The blackness on the windshield moved. The blackness was blood.

Crew rushed forward. He looked in through the passenger door. Crew winced, the reek of blood rushing up his nostrils.

"Jesus," he said, staring at the remains of the driver. His belly had been torn open, the guts in there steaming. One of his legs clung to his body by ribbons of flesh. His arms, held over his face, were mangled and broken.

Crew staggered away. He raced around to the passenger side and almost tripped over the body. It had been Renfrew. His head, at least, was intact; but the rest of him was shredded. Pieces of the secret service chief littered the ground. His blood saturated the soil.

Crew stumbled toward the other cars and found a similar scene: the men had been ripped apart; their blood and their flesh festooned the trees and the grass.

The stink made Crew retch. His stomach heaved up a sandwich he'd eaten that afternoon. He fell to his knees, panting. Saliva drooled from his mouth.

He heard a clunk; something landing on a car roof. He turned toward the noise. Crew got to his feet and dizziness swam over him.

"Steady, there," said the boy, squatting on top of Renfrew's car. The youth was naked.

Crew aimed his gun at him. "What the hell happened here? Tell me, or I'll kill you, and then I'll find your father and your mother, and I'll kill them, too."

"They're right behind you, Brit."

Crew spun round.

Two colossal black-furred creatures glared at him through yellow animal eyes. Crew gasped and loosened his grip on the gun. The creatures stood on two legs. The legs bent backwards like horse's legs. They had heads like dogs or ... or wolves, and their arms hung low at their flanks. Claws arced from their fingers. They snarled at Crew, revealing their long, sharp canines.

He went to shoot.

Something hit him from the right, knocking the wind out of him. He scrabbled around, grabbing for the gun but the gun was gone. He looked up and saw what hit him.

"Shit," he said, leaping to his feet, stumbling away from the monster.

The boy laughed. "That's my Uncle Willie, and them over there" – he pointed, and Crew looked. Four wolf-headed beasts appeared from the trees, snarling and crouching as if ready to pounce – "are the Connellys from Patrick Street. And then there's…"

And he kept gesturing, and Crew kept turning to see what he was pointing at, and soon enough the British interrogator found himself corralled by creatures he couldn't name; dozens of them, lethal and drooling.

Crew fell to his knees. He shivered and started to whimper. He thought about his boys and about his wife and tears welled in his eyes. He tried to speak but his mouth was dry, and fear had clogged up his throat.

The boy, still squatting on top of the car, said, "Will they send someone looking for you, Mr Crew? Like they sent you to look for the soldiers? Like they've always sent someone to look for soldiers, and travelers, and traders, and monks, and ancient Celtic priests, and long-lost kings. People always go missing in these parts, Mr Crew. It's border country. We're a different breed out here." He smiled. "Animals, you see. No compassion. No conscience. No regrets."

A howl made Crew start. One of the beasts had turned its face to the sky and was calling, and the call echoed over the wilderness. And then the other creatures looked up at the night and howled.

Crew clapped his hands over his ears. He rolled up into a little ball. The boy on the car leapt down and by the time his feet hit the ground he'd turned into what his parents were; what his Uncle Willie was; what the Connellys had become.

And he charged at Crew and Crew screamed as the clawed and canined monster ploughed into him.

Crew tried to fight but he was weak against the beast. The howling that had deafened Crew turned into snarls and growls. The village of monsters closed on him and fell on him and devoured him.

# In Sorrow Thou Shalt Bring Forth Children

THE ELEVATOR JERKED, AND the lights flickered. Jessup gasped, and a shudder passed through him.

"Wish it wouldn't do that," he said, gaze flitting around the elevator, "I hate these things."

Confined spaces gave him the creeps. Buried alive and all that Poe crap. A sweat broke out on the back of his neck. He tugged at his shirt collar to let some air in, but the air in here was humid.

"Come on, come on."

The elevator hummed its way down. It clanked and jerked. Jessup cursed and reached out an arm to steady himself. This is getting reported, he thought; and the maintenance guy's getting fired. Whoever he was, he should be on the phone to the elevator firm every day, stalking the hell out of them, threatening to kidnap their kids unless they get down here and fix this box of string and glue.

The elevator bumped and pinged its arrival in the underground parking lot. Jessup blew air out of his cheeks. The doors slid open.

"Damn."

He'd forgotten how dark it was in the parking lot. He squinted, peering into the gloom. He made out the pillars. He made out other shapes lurking in the blackness. He didn't know what they were – trash cans, old TV sets, refrigerators, shopping carts, ghosts.

Jessup chuckled and shook his head; told himself not to be such an asshole. He stepped out into the darkness, eyes fixed on the pool of light a hundred yards ahead of him. The light fanned out of a bulb hanging from the parking lot's low ceiling. It was the only source of illumination in this damn hole in the ground. Walk straight through that luminous pool, he thought, and I'm at the Toyota – and I can get the hell out of here.

He took a few steps then stopped. Hold on, he thought, and took out his cell phone. He stood in the dark and dialled.

"Maintenance," said a craggy voice.

"Yeah, this is Mike Jessup – "

"From Rittle & Brande?"

"From Rittle & Brande, that's right."

"Everything okay, there? You seen all the apartments, now?"

"Uh, yeah – what's your name?"

"My name?"

"Yes, your name."

"My name's Isaac."

"Isaac. You're maintenance guy here, right?"

"Sure am. Maintain; that's what I do."

"Well, you need to maintain better if you want to keep your job, Isaac. Do you want to keep your job?"

Silence, and Isaac breathing.

Jessup said, "You heard me all right up there?"

"I heard you all right, Mr Jessup. And, yeah, I need my job."

"Good. Let's get you doing it, then. It's the elevator, Isaac. It's, uh, clunky. Jerks a lot, and the light flickers."

"Yeah, it's old. Like me. I'm clunky, too. Jerk a lot. You get like that when you're old, that's all."

"Well, that's not good enough. We've got people coming in an out over the next few weeks. Rittle & Brande's refurbishment guys. Architects, surveyors, construction foremen, exterminators. They can't work with clunky and jerky, Isaac. Rittle & Brande can't work with clunky and jerky."

He heard Isaac breathe again, and after a few seconds Isaac said, "They ain't gonna want me, then?"

"That's not what I said. What I said is that these elevators, they need maintaining. You need to be on the phone with the elevator people – "

"The elevator people, they ain't there anymore. I told you, Mr Jessup: everything's old."

Jessup tilted his head from side to side. "Yeah, well, you need to find some elevator maintenance guys. Check the Yellow Pages. We can't have people getting stuck in the elevator, Isaac."

"No one's ever got stuck in those elevators. Not since I been here. And that's forty years. They're clunky, maybe, but they ain't never given up."

"That's good to hear. But you can never tell. I want it seen to, so see to it. Rittle & Brande will need a maintenance guy here when this place is spruced up and the rich folk are living here, throwing tips around. You could be that guy, Isaac. But you need to clean up – "

"And not be clunky and jerky."

"Yeah, not be clunky and jerky – oh, and Isaac..."

"Yes, Mr Jessup."

"We need another light source in the parking lot. It's an abyss down here. I can't see a thing. People can get hurt in the dark."

Isaac made a noise and it sounded like he'd said, "Yeah," but Jessup didn't hear properly and said, "What's that?"

"Nothing."

"What about the light, then?"

"It's always been dark down there."

"Always just came to an end, Isaac. There's no always anymore. It's all change, now. Everything's new." He waited, then said, "Okay?"

"Sure. But you know..."

"Know what, Isaac?"

The maintenance man hesitated, and Jessup wanted him off the phone.

He said, "Is there a problem, Isaac? Because if there is we can – "

"It's just ... the kids."

"The kids?"

"They always played down there. Down there in the dark."

"The kids."

"Yeah, the kids."

"There are no kids, Isaac. There are no residents. The building's been empty ten years – rats and spiders and old TVs, that's all."

"The kids, though."

"You're talking about neighborhood kids?"

Silence again. Jessup imagined Isaac's brain going around and around, grinding out an answer.

The maintenance man said, "I just mean kids. General, like."

Jessup tutted. "They shouldn't be playing here, whoever they are. It's private property. Rittle & Brande own it, now, Isaac. That's why we put signs out front saying, 'Rittle & Brande. Private property. Do not enter'." He blew air out of his cheeks and wiped his brow. Then he said, "If you know of any kids that play here, Isaac, you'd better tell them to stay away, find another garbage dump. Is that clear, now? I'm holding you responsible."

Isaac sighed. Jessup furrowed his brow. He didn't like the noise Isaac just made. He couldn't say why he didn't like it, he just didn't, so he let it go and said, "Is that clear with you, Isaac?"

"Yes, Mr Jessup, guess it has to be."

"Yes, it does have to be. You get on it, Isaac. Elevator, kids – you deal with it all and I'll be in touch later in the week. I may drop by to see how you're doing. Do it right and I'll put in a good word for you with the hiring and firing guys."

Isaac's voice came down the phone, saying, "You be c – ", but Jessup cut him off. He smiled and thought: have the last word, then slam the phone down on them; gives you the edge.

He slipped the cell into his jacket pocket and strode towards the light. He'd suggest to Rittle & Brande they get rid of Isaac. Forty years – that's a good, long while to be at the same job. Time he scuttled off. Rittle & Brande could find a place for him in one of their retirement homes. Isaac could die there among his own kind; among the old and the "always" brigade.

It's always raining in town.

It's always busy on the subway.

It's always been dark down there.

Jessup stopped. The pool of light lay ten yards ahead. He narrowed his eyes. What was that? he thought, convinced he'd heard a noise off to his left.

"Hello?" he said, and the darkness threw the word back at him, making it bounce off the concrete walls.

Jessup shivered. That must've been it, he thought – an echo. Maybe my footsteps. He blew air out of his cheeks and shook his head, thinking, You're such a chicken-shit, Mickey.

He walked on and stepped into the light, and the tennis ball lobbed out of the darkness ahead of him.

Jessup stopped and his nerves tightened. Chills leached through his veins and he felt a sweat break out across his back.

The ball bounced past him. He turned to follow its course. It fell into the darkness, the plop-plop as it struck the concrete fading out into silence.

Jessup faced front again. He stared into the shadows. He swallowed, his Adam's apple bobbing in his throat. He started to speak, but he had no voice. He coughed, clearing the debris from his gullet.

"Who ... who's there?" If there was anybody there, they didn't answer. Jessup said, "Don't mess with me. I do taekwondo."

He didn't do taekwondo, but Candice started classes last week and said he should come, lose some of that flab. But he never would. Not unless something happened. Something like this.

His legs felt shaky and he wanted to pee.

He said, "I'll phone the cops. You're ... you're not allowed in here, it's private property. You're trespassing. Rittle & Brande own it, now. You hear that? We own it and it's out of bounds. There's security. You won't be – "

He instinctively ducked, but the soccer ball wouldn't have hurt him. It looped out of the darkness and arced over his head. It bounced at the edge of the pool of light before bobbing off into the shadows.

Jessup's gaze darted around. He panted, his heart racing.

"Okay," he said, "I think we're done, now. Game's over. You win."

The Toyota lay twenty yards ahead of him. He couldn't see it, but he knew that's where he'd parked it. Problem was, the joker throwing the balls was also in front of him; and probably stood between Jessup and the car.

Jessup reached into his pocket for the cell phone. Cops'll deal with this, he thought; put the heebie-jeebies up these he kids. He started dialling 911 and didn't see the football spin out of the darkness on his right. It cracked into his wrist and he dropped the phone. Pain shot up his arm. He yelped and stumbled away. The football rolled out of the light.

Jessup cowered and said, "What the hell's going on? You've broken my wrist. I'll sue you. I'll have you thrown in jail. You hear me?"

Jessup flicked his hand about. His wrist wasn't broken but it hurt like hell. He squatted to pick up his phone. His eyes were fixed on the darkness.

This is not funny, he thought; not funny anymore.

Crouching, looking out for other missiles, he dialled 911 and put the phone to his ear.

Something cracked against the side of his head. He dropped the phone and toppled forward. For a moment he didn't know where he was. Then he came to. His brain throbbed with pain. He groaned and touched the back of his skull. A warm wetness matted his hair. He looked at his hand and saw the blood. He almost fainted but managed to keep himself together. He scrabbled around for his phone.

But then he froze.

The baseball bobbled gently from side to side a couple of feet away. Jessup grabbed it. He sat, legs stretched out in front of him. He studied the ball. A blob of blood – his blood – stained the surface.

Fury swelled in his breast. He clenched his teeth and he could feel the blood rush to his cheeks. He got up, ignoring the dizziness. He darted looks into the darkness and lobbed the baseball up and down in his palm.

"You want this back, huh? You want it back, you bastard? Well take it, then – and I hope it" – he pitched the baseball into the gloom – "kills you."

He heard the clip of bat on ball.

He gasped and ducked sharply. The baseball whizzed back over his head. It shot into the shadows behind Jessup and clanked against the elevator doors.

Jessup glared towards where he guessed the elevator would be. He breathed hard, sucking air into his lungs. Terror crawled over him. His skin poured sweat and pain pulsed through his head.

"Who are you?" he said, his voice high-pitched. Still crouching, he faced forward again. "Who the hell are you?"

Jessup tried to listen. Tried to hear breathing, or whispers, or giggling, or footsteps. But he heard nothing. He shut his eyes and dropped his head. He started to cry and that made him tremble.

"Let me get to my car," he said through his tears. "Let me go home, please let me go home."

He heard something hiss, and the hiss got louder, and the rock shot from the darkness. He dropped flat on the concrete and the rock flew over him. He leaped to his feet, anger chasing away the fear, and he said, "What the hell are you doing? You could've killed me. Balls are one thing; but rocks – "

That hissing sound again. He cowered, curled up into a ball. The rock whipped in from his left. It glanced off his elbow and jarred. Jessup yelped and dropped to his knees. His eyes flitted around, trying to see. He panted, and his heart bumped against his ribs.

The phone trilled.

It was on the ground. He dived for it and answered it while lying flat on his stomach. He didn't wait to hear who it was, just said, "For God's sake, help me. They're throwing stones at me. They'll kill me. Phone the cops, please phone the – "

"Mr Jessup, sir?"

"Isaac?"

"Oh, Mr Jessup."

"Isaac, phone the cops. The kids, it's the kids, they're throwing stuff at me, Isaac. Baseballs, soccer balls – and now, they're throwing stones."

"Oh, Mr Jessup, I'm sorry."

"You will be unless you phone the cops."

"Cops can't do nothing."

"Cops can't – what are you talking about?"

"Last time we was on the phone."

"Just now."

"Just now, yeah. I was about to tell you, Mr Jessup, to be careful but you hung up on me."

"Yeah, look, whatever – phone the cops, Isaac."

"I said cops can't do nothing."

Jessup gasped. Anger boiled in his veins. He got up into a crouch and said, "Get down here, Isaac, and get these kids off of me."

Isaac hesitated, and then said, "Can't do that."

"Can't do – you do what I say, asshole. Get here and tell these kids that I'll have them locked up for the rest of their lives unless they let me get to my car."

"Mr Jessup," said Isaac, a tremble in his voice, "it ain't like that. You can't lock 'em up, sir. They ain't – they – they ain't – "

The rock struck Jessup in the arm. He dropped the phone and scurried away. His arm ached, and he rubbed it, saying, "That hurts, you bastards."

A second rock came whistling out of the darkness behind him. He ducked, but the missile's trajectory was low, and it whacked his thigh.

Jessup hopped about rubbing his leg. He said, "Okay, that's enough."

He bent down and picked up the rock. It was heavy and jagged, the size of an orange. He tossed it and it clunked against metal. Jessup cursed, knowing he'd probably dented the Toyota.

Two rocks flew past his head, one from the right, one from the left.

"Where are you? Where are you, you little – "

He saw the rock coming but stood frozen. It smashed into his chest and sent him reeling. A jolt of pain burst through his breast and for a few moments he struggled to breathe. He rubbed his chest and started to cry, saying, "Stop now, please."

A tinny voice drew his attention. He looked at the phone. Isaac still spoke to him, thinking he was listening. Jessup bounded to the phone and snatched it up. He put it to his ear and heard Isaac saying, "... so there's nothing I can do, Mr Jessup. We're all powerless, here – that's how it's always been," and then Isaac hung up.

"Isaac ... Isaac ... Isaac, damn you, where – "

The rock cracked against his skull. Pain shot through his head. Stars erupted in front of his eyes. He stumbled backwards, arms out. His knees buckled, and he almost fell but managed to keep his balance. Blood poured from his forehead. He blinked it out of his eyes. He touched his head and saw his hand.

He screamed.

"Stop this, stop this, stop – "

And the whistle of stones made him cover his head. But too many showered towards him. They struck his body and he screeched, leaping about trying to avoid them. He ran this way and that way, trying to find cover. But the stones came from every direction, containing him in the pool of light. The pain was dreadful.

Stones broke his arms so he couldn't raise them to protect his head and face. He begged them to stop but he got smashed in the cheek, and then the ear, and the shoulder, and then everywhere – all over his body.

He fell to his knees. He stared at the concrete. They pelted him, their missiles thudding against him. Blood spilled from him and splashed on the ground. He wailed, the agony unbearable.

The stones rained on him. The darkness fell on him.

Shapes, he thought, his mind slipping away; shapes lurking in the blackness – trash cans, old TV sets, refrigerators, shopping carts, ghosts ...

# When Soft Voices Die

"EXCUSE ME," SAID EDNA.

The youth didn't respond.

"Excuse me," she said again.

His eyes were shut and his mouth was open. He was sleeping. The plugs were stuffed into his ears. The music – if you could call it music – droned from the tiny machine tucked into his jeans.

Edna leaned closer. Her arthritis ached, a surge of pain clambering up her spine. She grimaced and hissed in a breath. She caught the youth's odour: stale beer and last night's curry.

"Oh dear." She twisted her face away.

She wafted a hand in front of her nose and glanced again at the boy. He was seventeen or eighteen, maybe. His skin was pale and peppered with acne. He was thin and bony. His Adam's apple bobbed like a buoy as he slept. One of his front teeth was missing and the rest were tobacco-stained.

She tried again, her voice firmer this time. "Excuse me, young man."

He didn't respond

"Try again, Edna."

Edna turned towards Jane. Her sister was peeking from between the seats. "You come out of your hiding place and try," said Edna.

"You're the eldest, you have to do it. Mother gave it to you. Poke him. Poke him in the arm."

"I can't poke him. You can't poke people."

"Poke the lout."

"You come over here and poke him."

"Oh, Edna. Wake him up. Tell him to switch that thing off, or at least turn it down. This is his last chance. If he doesn't listen, you know what to do."

"Tell the guard again?"

"What good did that do?" said Jane. "No one listens anymore. No one pays heed."

It was true. The world was ill mannered; people were rude; everyone had a couldn't-be-bothered attitude.

This youth – who epitomised ill mannered, rude, and couldn't-be-bothered – had been travelling on the 07:13 for the past two weeks. Every day he trudged onto the train, wearing a scowl and a hoodie. The plugs were already in his ears, the tinny music thump-thumping away. The volume was loud enough for Edna to hear the words, the ugly, brutal, murderous words.

That first day, the man in the suit – Edna didn't know his name; you didn't know names these days – rose from his seat at the rear of the carriage and tottered over to the youth. The man leaned forward and asked – nicely enough – if the teenager could turn down his music. The boy's scowl deepened – and he snapped his head into the suited man's face. The poor fellow keeled over. Blood pulsed from his broken nose. Edna's bowels seemed to fill with ice water. The dryness in her throat turned a scream into a croak. She gripped the back of the seat in front and thought about getting up, going to help the man in the suit. But she didn't – her legs felt too heavy; her fear too strong.

The poor fellow, his nose spilling blood, struggled to his feet and reached into his pocket for his mobile. He seemed to be dialling, but his hand shook so much he could barely handle the phone, let alone press specific keys. Grabbing the mobile from his victim's hand, the youth – who had not bothered to remove the plugs from his ears – glowered, and said, "You phone the cops, I'll find out where you live and I'll batter you, and your wife, and your kids." He hurled the phone down the carriage. It struck a window and clattered to the floor near the toilet.

Seven other passengers shared the carriage. They did nothing. The man staggered down the aisle, his eyes starting to bruise. He picked up his mobile and tried to pin it back together, but his hands were shaking. Edna made to stand up and help him, but Jane clutched her arm and gave her a "don't-get-involved" look. The man stumbled back to his seat. Tears rolled down his cheeks and he carried on fumbling with his broken phone.

For two weeks they put up with the youth's music. Those eight passengers suffered in silence, each one, maybe, hoping that another would beg the teenager to turn the volume down on his machine. No one did. They each sunk deeper into their own worlds. And that was the way they liked it, thank you very much: heads down to focus on a novel, a sudoku puzzle, a crossword, anything, anything at all that would act as a flimsy barrier between their world and the worlds of others.

They could have moved carriages, of course. But habits are hard to break. Changing a ritual is sometimes more terrifying than facing a monster. And anyway, there were only two carriages on the 07:13. It was a six-stop train, and all the passengers had their favourite seats. So they put up with it and hoped they could reach journey's end without a confrontation.

For two weeks. Until yesterday. When Jane broke the ceasefire.

"I can't bear it any longer," she said, getting out of her seat. Using the headrests on the seats as support, she hobbled towards the teenager. Edna cringed as she watched her sister shuffle along the trembling floor of the carriage. She and Jane had made this train journey every day for twenty years. They had three-stops: a pleasant, brief jaunt through a rushing, rural landscape.

"Look here, young man," said Jane when, after a good half-minute, she got to where he was sitting. "We would all be very grateful if you could show some manners and turn that thing down. We've no interest in hearing your music."

From her seat, Edna saw that the youth appeared to cough into Jane's face. Jane flinched and turned away from the teenager. She bowed her head and rubbed at her mouth with a handkerchief.

Edna strained to see what had happened to her sister. Her heart bumped against her breast, and her entrails squirmed. What terrible thing had that boy done? What injury had he caused dear Jane?

Edna got up and stepped into the aisle.

"Jane?" she said as her sister came towards her.

Jane raised her head. Tears threaded down her cheeks. Phlegm oozed from her spectacles. Edna gasped and opened her arms to hug her. But Jane she brushed past and went to her seat. Edna trundled back and sat next to her sister.

Jane took off her glasses and said, "Couldn't see to get back here without them so I had to leave them on." She wiped the lenses clean with her handkerchief. "There's none on my face is there?"

Edna shook her head. She linked arms with Jane and Jane trembled, saying, "He is dirty and vile, and we shall tell Mother."

Edna gazed through the window and saw things change: green became grey, fields became concrete, sky became buildings, and Edna thought about the terrors Mother would wreak.

---

Anyone asking Edna and Jane where they were headed each a morning was always surprised by the response.

"We're going to visit Mother."

"Really? Your – Mother? If you don't mind me asking, how – "

Edna would say, "I'm eighty-six."

Jane would say, "And I'm eighty-four."

"And your mother?"

Mother was a hundred-and-seven and stick-sharp. "Young people," she would say to her daughters, her Romanian accent still thick despite living in Britain for over sixty years. "I not understand. Trains. Ha! We walk everywhere. Walking, that is how we travel. Walking and horse." She would flap her bony hand dismissively and say, "Youth. Youth is lazy."

The house smelled of incense and age. Candles flickered on the mantlepiece, casting a dancing light over the living room. Edna and Jane sat on the sofa, which was covered in a purple and black silk throw. Mother was sunk into her favourite chair. Cushions pressed into her on both sides. It seemed that they held her up like traction. The Seer, Mother's cat, purred at the old woman's feet.

"… and then we went to the Women's Institute where they had this marvellous talk by this marvellous man. He'd been doing voluntary work in Africa. He had all these wonderful pictures, all these smiling, happy children. Oh, it was – "

Mother snored.

"Mother? Are you sleeping," said Edna, irritated that her story had been interrupted.

"No. I am tired of nonsense."

"Nonsense? It's not – "

Mother held up a hand. Her fingers were like twigs. "Jane, my daughter, Jane, why are you sad and quiet today? You are child with the rattling tongue."

Edna said, "Jane's feeling under the – "

"It's that young man on the train, Mother," said Jane.

"The boy with music box?"

Edna said, "It's called an iPod."

Jane said, "He spat in my face today."

Mother made a clicking sound in her throat. The skin on her face tightened. Her dark, dark eyes narrowed, and her lips became like a piece of thread on her face.

Edna felt her face grow red. "It's all very unfortunate," she said. "Maybe we should report him again."

"Fat lot of good that did," said Jane.

Edna saw that Jane had locked eyes with Mother, and Mother was understanding everything and concocting something terrible in her ancient mind.

Edna, knowing this would not be good, said, "We could write a letter to the train company, couldn't we."

"Yes, we could do that," said Jane. "We could sit around and let nasty people like him walk all over us. We could grin and bear it, Edna. We could let them spit in our faces day after day after day."

Jane took out her handkerchief and blew her nose. Her eyes were red. Edna dropped her gaze to her hands, which were folded in her lap. Jane was right: something had to be done; but that something, when Mother was involved, could be hideous. Edna only wanted the boy scolded; told not to travel on their train again; made to walk wherever he was going. But hate welled in Jane's heart. She would ask for anguish, and Mother would provide it.

Mother said, "This boy, he love his music."

"I don't call it music," said Jane.

"It seems he can't be without it," said Edna.

Mother pushed herself to her feet. "Then he shall not." She shuffled through to the kitchen. The old woman started to chant.

---

Edna poked the teenager.

His eyes snapped open and he raised his head from the window. He scowled at Edna and his expression was so harsh that she had to take a step backwards.

She tried to speak, but nothing came out. She swallowed, and then tried again. "Could you, would you be so kind as to turn your music down, please. It's, well, we can all of us hear it, you see. And we really don't want to hear it."

He tugged at one of the thin, white cables. A tiny earplug dropped from his ear.

"What?"

Edna flinched. It was as if he'd thrown the word at her.

"The music. We can all hear it. We'd be grateful if you could – "

"So what? I don't give a shit. It's a free country. Why don't you go sit down before you fall down, you stupid old bitch."

Edna's bladder chilled and her knees buckled. She tightened her frail muscles and made her hands into fists. "You spat in my sister's face."

"I'll spit in your face, too, if you don't sit down. Witch."

"Please. This really is your last chance."

He leaned forward and showed his teeth. "No, bitch, it's yours. Now piss off."

He popped the plug back into his ear. He turned the volume up and made the music louder than it had ever been during this awful fortnight. He rested his head against the window again and shut his eyes.

Edna sighed, and her shoulders slumped. She reached into her pocket and took out the vial. It contained a clear blue liquid. Edna looked at the youth. Her heart felt heavy. Had he only showed some respect; some courtesy.

"There would have been no need for this," she said.

Edna uncorked the vial.

After chanting and producing something that smelled of burning flesh, Mother had come out of the kitchen, a mist of steam in her wake. She handed the vial of blue liquid to Edna. She said, "The boy, he shall always have his music." Mother sagged into her chair and fell asleep.

Edna said, "Young man," and he swore and looked up, scowling. She tossed the liquid in his face.

He flapped his hands about his head. He spluttered and rubbed his eyes. Edna took a step back. Her throat was dry and her legs felt weak. The boy raged, and it frightened her. She glanced at Jane, then looked back at the youth. He sprang to his feet and said, "What do you think you're doing, you stupid old cow?"

His words slipped away. Edna's stare was fixed on the wires that snaked from his ears. She blinked, clearing her vision, making sure she wasn't seeing things.

The youth looked at her and said, "Did you hear me, witch?"

"Oh my, my," said Edna.

He lunged at her saying, "Did you hear – ?", and then he stopped and grimaced.

"I don't believe it," said Edna.

"What's happening?" It was Jane. She'd tottered down the carriage.

"Ow, ow, ow," said the boy, sitting down, "what's going on?"

Edna said, "My, my, isn't that amazing."

Jane, also staring at the iPod's cables, said, "They've changed colour."

The youth yelled. The other passengers had gathered to see. "What's happened?" said the man with bruised eyes.

Edna said, "He's learning some manners."

The boy screamed again, and Edna faced him. He plucked at one of the cables and squealed. The plug wouldn't come out of his ear. It was stuck there, like a finger is stuck on to a hand; like a hand is stuck on to an arm – it is part of it. And the plugs, the cables that dangled from them, the machine itself held in the youth's hand, had become part of him. They had melded into flesh and attached themselves to him. He was human and iPod, evolved. He stared at his palm where the machine had created a rectangle of flesh, and then he looked up at Edna.

He said, "Make it stop. What's going on?"

"You should've thought of that when we asked you to turn it down," said Edna.

He looked at her, tears streaming down his face, and said, "What?" his voice a falsetto, "What?"

"He can't hear you," said the man with bruised eyes.

"No change there, then."

The boy with the iPod growing out of his head screamed for the music to stop.

— • —

# Kings & Paupers

GUY DASHED THROUGH THE station doors. He stopped in the waiting room and looked around. The ticket office was closed, a shutter drawn over the hatch.

The waiting room smelled old and mouldy. Damp stained the peach-coloured walls, and the paint peeled like sunburned skin.

Guy caught his breath. "Hello?" he said.

He looked down at himself. He was soaked and he was muddy.

"Hello?" he said again.

Guy tutted. He could wait forever for someone to come. He looked around, then vaulted the ticket gate, and bounded down the stairs. He pushed through a set of double doors, and out on to the neat, empty, Victorian-style platform.

He looked for a sign naming the station, but he couldn't see one.

He looked at his watch. The hands were still. He tapped the watch face with his finger. He brought the watch up to his ear. He tried to wind it, but the hands wouldn't spin. He tapped the watch again. The watch stayed stopped. He checked the time on his mobile, but the phone was dead. Guy flapped his arms and cursed.

"Lost, sir?"

## THOMAS EMSON

Guy turned. The guard strolled down the platform. He was a thin man with thin lips and dark eyes on chalk-white skin.

"I need to get to London," said Guy. He stepped towards the guard but stopped and flinched when an odour saturated his nostrils. It smelled like decay. Guy coughed, then said, "When's the next train?"

"Soon," said the guard.

"Which platform?" Guy looked across to the opposite platform. Slats of wood hung from the roof. Windows were shattered. Newspapers flapped on the platform. Words in a language that Guy had never seen were graffitied on the walls in brash strokes of red and black.

"This platform," said the guard. "Best you stay on this side."

"Is there a timetable? I need to work out a route."

"There's one train, sir. It goes this way," said the guard, pointing. "And there's another train." The guard pointed towards the mouth of a tunnel.

"All right. I need a ticket. A single to London."

The guard raised his eyebrows. His forehead stayed smooth. "No ticket?"

"I was in a hurry. I had an accident up the road. I'm an MP, and I have to be in Parliament tonight for a debate."

"It happened quickly, then."

"What did?"

"The accident. Quickly."

"Yes, it did."

The guard narrowed his dark eyes until they were dark slits on his pale face. "You'll just have to take your chances."

Guy glared at the guard and clenched his fists. He turned away and strode down the platform. When the heat left his face and the rage in his chest died out, he went back to the guard. Guy held out his mobile. "Is there a phone I could use? My battery's flat. I need to tell them I may be late."

"There is no phone."

Guy shuddered. The anger ignited in his breast again. "Don't you know who I am?" he said.

"No I don't, sir. But it doesn't matter who you are. The train's the train, and it's the same train for everyone. Kings and paupers. All the same. And you've got to get on if you want to get to where you're going, sir."

Guy rolled his eyes and grunted.

He turned around and went to go through the double doors that led to the stairs, but there were no doors. Only a brick wall covered in moss and damp.

He stared at the wall, his mouth open.

He had words he wanted to say but they cowered in his throat, and his Adam's apple bobbed as he tried to shove them out. Guy pressed his hand flat against the wall, and the wall was cold and wet.

Something wailed in the tunnel. It sounded more animal than mechanical. The guard said, "That could be your train."

Guy closed his eyes and put his hand to his brow. He was shaking, his heart thudding against his breast. There was a door, there was a ...

Guy tried to retrace his steps, how he got here. He thought about himself driving through the rain. He should have slowed down. But he didn't, and he lost control and skidded on the wet road. The bend lunged at him. He crashed into a tree. He remembered the noise, and his head jerking forwards and cracking the windscreen. The steering wheel thumped his chest, and a moment of black silence devoured him.

He came to and got out of the car. He looked up and down the road. He saw the sign. It was pressed into a bramble bush. The word was written in red capital letters on a once-white background. It said station ¼. Guy ran, lashed by rain.

The train slid out of the tunnel, growling and coughing smoke. It was an old steam engine. Guy smelled the decay again as the train burned its fuel. He pressed his palm to his temple.

"Headache, sir? You look a bit..."

The screaming of brakes drowned the guard's voice.

The train was black and long. The windows were tinted. The doors were the old-fashioned type with handles you had to wrench down.

One of the doors opened, and a guard stepped out. He looked like the station guard, with his dark eyes and his chalk-white face.

The train guard looked at Guy. "Got your ticket, sir?"

"This one hasn't got a ticket," said the station guard.

The train guard raised his eyebrows. His forehead stayed smooth. "No ticket? You understand it's a 'purchase-in-advance' service, don't you, sir?"

Guy scowled. "Obviously not. This is ridiculous. Where's the exit? There were double doors. I need to–" He shook his head and tutted. This was a nightmare, of course. He was unconscious and would soon wake up in hospital, Millie sobbing over him.

The station guard said, "I've told him he'll have to take his chances."

The train guard folded his arms. "He will." He moved aside so Guy could get on the train. "Are you getting on? We've not got forever."

Guy felt bewildered. He glanced at the brick wall, and then at the station guard. Without thinking, he stepped on the train. His eyes brushed over the train's sleek interiors. Passageways led off towards the front and rear. Compartment doors were embossed with gold figurines. Guy breathed, and the aroma of roses drenched his nostrils.

The train guard shut the door and it became darker inside the train. Guy looked at the guard. His eyes were fluorescent blue. He smiled, but the skin of his cheeks did not crease.

The train chugged and jerked and started to move. Guy and the guard swayed as the train picked up speed.

The guard went down the corridor and gestured for Guy to follow. The guard stopped and opened a compartment door. The inside of the door was lined with purple velvet. He signalled for Guy to enter the compartment.

The seats were lined with purple velvet. The window looked out over fields peppered with what might have been scarecrows: rags of things pinned up on poles. The train moved too fast for Guy to define them. He narrowed his eyes and felt lost. This land was strange to him. He watched it sweep by and tried to remember it, but this was somewhere he'd never seen before.

"Have a pleasant journey, sir," said the guard, and shut the door.

Guy put his briefcase down. He perched on the edge of a seat. He shook his head. He should have asked how long the journey would take.

The train jerked, and Guy jerked with it. The engine picked up speed and made the outside world a blur. Guy held his breath and grabbed the armrests. His body prepared for G-forces to pull at him. But instead everything felt smooth, like he was floating. The blurred world zoomed past the window. Guy felt dazed. He put his head in his hands and closed his eyes.

The brakes screeched. The train stuttered. Guy looked up. The train stopped. Guy stood, and he tried the door, but the door was jammed.

He turned to look out of the window. His eyes went wide, and he opened his mouth.

Another train had stopped next to his train. He looked through its cracked and grimy windows. Passengers raced up and down the aisle. Their mouths were open in silent screams. They flapped their hands about their heads trying to ward off the black forms swooping about the carriage. Scratching and tearing at the passengers, these creatures had fiery gashes for eyes, and their contours were outlined in flickering flames.

A fat woman with tattoos on her arms caught Guy looking. She pressed herself against the window. Terror stretched her face. Her mouth shaped the words help me! help me! A black thing fell on her shoulders, its fiery fingers clawing at her eyes. She thrashed about and made a screaming shape with her mouth. The creature raised its head and stared at Guy and Guy felt his insides turn icy and melt away.

Guy's strength leached out of him, and he gripped a handrail to stop himself falling.

A whistle blew. Guy's train lurched forward tossing him across the compartment. He saw the other train rush into a blur of black and red and specks of fire.

Guy went to the door. He yanked at the handle.

"Let me out. Let me out of here."

The door opened, and Guy stepped back as the guard entered the compartment. A bundle of newspapers was tucked under his arm. He scowled, and said, "You settle down and hope that you're on the right train. You've seen what the other train's like."

He held out a folded newspaper. Guy took it. The guard tipped his cap and left the compartment.

Guy sat down and unfolded the paper. He stared at a picture of himself on the front page and the headline beneath it saying, MP KILLED IN CRASH.

# Sequence

"You loved your wife so much, you stabbed her" – Munroe glanced at the sheet of paper on the desk – "thirty-five times. That's love, is it?"

Fisher put his head in his hands. He started to cry again, trembling as the tears came. The guy looked a mess. Sweat darkened his pink shirt. His hair stuck up like wheat in a field. The man stank; he needed a shower.

Munroe stood and turned to face the two-way mirror. He put his hands in his pockets and fumbled with his badge and his house keys. He shrugged into the two-way, then glanced at the clock above it: one forty-two p.m. He faced Fisher.

"Your wife having an affair, Mr Fisher?"

Fisher scowled. "No."

"How d'you know?"

"I just know."

"How can you be so certain?"

Fisher stared at him. "How can you be so certain that your wife's not having an affair, Detective?"

It was like a punch in the chest. He glared at Fisher and gave the fury time to die out; gave the hate time to flush his veins and thin out in his blood.

He was cool again and said, "Was she having an affair?"

Fisher put his face back in his hands and said, "No, she wasn't."

Munroe sat down and rested his elbows on the table. "And then there's the kids."

Fisher leaned back in his chair and his face stretched out in pain. He put his hands in his hair and wailed. He slumped forward, resting his forehead on his arms and he wept again. "Please," he said.

"Is that what your kids said? 'Please, daddy. Please don't kill us like you killed mommy'."

Fisher trembled. "I didn't... I didn't... I ..."

"Didn't do it?"

"Didn't mean to."

Munroe slapped the desk, and Fisher jerked.

"You didn't mean to?" said Munroe. "You see, Mr Fisher: that's really hard to take in. I'll tell you why it's hard to take in: a man who 'didn't mean to' wouldn't stab his wife – whom he loved, and who wasn't sleeping around – thirty-five time with a" – he looked at the paper – "bread knife, before stabbing" – another glance at the sheet – "Charlie and Jennifer a total of twenty-eight times. It's not like your hand slipped, is it, Mr Fisher."

Blood coated the Fishers' kitchen. It poured down the walls, it seeped into the grooves between floor tiles, it pooled on the sink. Its odour soaked the air when Munroe and his colleagues had kicked down the back door at nine a.m.

## THOMAS EMSON

"Shit," said Munroe when he saw Ellen Fisher sprawled on the bloody floor. She was drenched in blood. Wounds gashed her body. "Shit, shit, no," said Munroe when he saw Charlie and Jennifer Fisher, saturated in blood, huddled dead near the kitchen door. "Put the weapon down, sir, and put your hands above your head," said Munroe when he saw Paul Fisher kneeling in the blood, knife in his left hand, cell phone in his right.

The next-door neighbor made the call. She heard screams at eight thirty-three a.m., peeped over the back fence, and saw Fisher kneeling in the kitchen.

Munroe had seen bloodbaths, but this topped them all. The kids made it bad for him. The boy was ten, the girl eight. Same ages as Ryan and Troy.

When they got back to the precinct, Chief Albeck waited. Blood vessels mapped his cheeks. Sweat stained the armpits of his blue-and-white striped shirt. His belly strained at the buttons. Hands on hips, gun holstered at his waist, he looked like an armed bull waiting to charge. Albeck had been a victim of crime himself a couple of days ago. His demeanor had gone from his usual "furious" to "homicidal". Munroe guessed Albeck would've sent a jaywalker to the chair that morning.

Albeck, snorting like that bull again, said, "I want him cracked and fried by five, Munroe. Is that clear?"

Albeck didn't wait for an answer. He turned and made his way upstairs. A policewoman had to press herself against the banister to make room for the chief. Sweat slicked the back of Albeck's neck. Without turning, he said, "It's the seventh one this morning across the city. I want to be first with a charge, Munroe."

Munroe got up again and looked into the two-way. He made a drinking gesture with his hand. He jangled the house keys in his pocket and thought of home. His heart bumped hard. Albeck had said five. But he'd be happy to have Fisher dealt with by six p.m. so he could weekend it with the boys. He only saw them twice a month, and never let work get in the way. That's why he lost them, and Susan, in the first place. "You're never home, so you won't notice if we're gone," she said eight months ago.

He looked up at the clock: two-ten p.m. He made the drinking signal again hoping Tommassi, Lewis, or Crown, would hoist their lazy asses down to the machine and get him a coffee.

It was an easy case: they had the whodunit; it was the whydunit he wanted.

Munroe dragged the chair back from the desk and sat down. He dumped his feet on the table. Fisher leaned back in his seat and looked at the detective.

"So you're in insurance," said Munroe, like it was dull; like it was not the kind of job a wife-and-kids-killer would be doing. "And your wife loves you, you love your wife; no one's sleeping with anyone behind anyone's back; the kids are doing great at school; the neighbors think you're apple pie." He threw out his arms. "Why d'you kill your family, Mr Fisher?"

"I told you."

"You told me, but you didn't expect me to believe that crap, did you? Come on, Fisher: that was the panic version; it's time to give me the between-you-and-me version, now."

"I've told you what happened. I waived my right to an attorney, Detective."

Fisher sobbed, his frame shuddering.

Munroe sympathized with the guy for a second: he was a father who'd lost his children. Munroe thought again: make that a father who'd killed his children; a father who'd butchered them; stabbed them – he pulled his feet off the desk, leaned forward, checked the sheet – twenty-eight times in total.

Munroe picked up the plastic evidence bag from the desk and dangled it in front of Fisher. "Do you think that by giving the judge some crazy 'it-wasn't-me-I-heard-voices-telling-me-to-do-it' crap you'll nail an insanity plea? Is that your thinking? Is that your insurance head doing the talking, Mr Fisher?"

"I'm not thinking that. I'm telling you the truth, detective. The cell phone rang, I answered it, and..." He shook his head, like he was trying to get rid of hornets in his hair.

"Stop doing that, you're making me dizzy," said Munroe. "And what? What happened when you answered it?" He put the evidence bag down on the desk.

Fisher said, "I was surprised it rang. It was new, and no one had the number and I thought it was switched off. Convinced it was switched off. I picked up and this voice ... a whisper ... said a number."

"What number?"

"The number five. And then he said other numbers. A sequence. I don't know how many, or what they were. I can't remember. Only the number five. And after he said 'Five', that's when ... Fisher moaned, "Oh God, oh God."

"What next?"

Fisher looked up at Munroe and said, "What next is that I'm on my knees, in my kitchen. Like you found me, Detective." They looked at each other. Fisher furrowed his brow. Munroe saw thinking going on behind the man's eyes. A cold sweat broke on the detective's nape. And then Fisher said, "In fact, I don't really know if I killed them. That's the truth, Detective, because I don't remember killing them. It wasn't like I was doing it."

"You confessed, Fisher."

"When did I confess?"

"In the – " Munroe stopped. He was going to say, "In the kitchen"; yeah, in the kitchen that morning – that's where Fisher confessed: before Munroe officially arrested him; before anything could be written down; before Munroe stared at the dead boy and thought of Ryan and of Troy and of the rage that their deaths would ignite in him.

Fisher's confession was piss in the wind.

Munroe looked at the bagged phone. It was a thin black thing, specks of blood on its blank screen. "Who called you?" he said.

"I don't know."

"You check the number?"

Fisher sagged back in his chair and threw his arms out. "Sorry, Detective, I was being arrested at the time. It wasn't a priority. And shouldn't that be your job? Haven't you done that?"

In the Fishers' kitchen that morning, Lewis had peeled back the guy's fingers and wrenched the phone from his hand. Munroe hoped his colleague had checked the cell before bagging it. He rubbed his brow and sighed. He thought about his sons and his heart felt heavy: their weekend together was fading away.

"Tell me why you did it, Fisher," he said, "then we can all go home."

"I can't."

"No, I guess you can't. You're in here for a while. Make it easy on yourself and co-operate." Munroe leaned back in the chair and folded his arms. "So: the cell rings."

"I answer it."

"You hear a voice."

"I hear the number five."

"Then a sequence of numbers which you cannot recall."

"That's right."

"And you kill your family."

"No... I don't... I felt as if I..." He clenched his teeth and he clenched his fists and he searched for the words. "I felt as if I ... lost myself. As if I ... slipped away."

Munroe curled his lip and stared at the man. "Do you hear voices, Fisher?"

"Voices?"

"Yeah, voices. Telling you to do stuff."

Fisher didn't answer.

Munroe said, "Seems I was right: we are going down the 'it-wasn't-me-I-heard-voices-telling-me-to-do-it' route."

Fisher stiffened his shoulders and tightened his face. His eyes narrowed, and he looked like someone standing in a door who wasn't going to move.

Munroe said, "Why are you doing this? You killed your wife and kids – "

"Maybe I didn't. Can't you see?"

"No, I can't see. An intruder would've left footprints in all that – " He was about to say "blood" but didn't. It made him think about the kids. He shook his head. "There's only you, Fisher."

"Maybe she did it."

Munroe stared at Fisher, and he could see the panic in the guy's eyes. "You're hanging on by your fingernails, Fisher. You can't avoid the fall, pal."

Fisher ignored Munroe and said, "Maybe she killed ... our children. And then killed herself."

"Did she have a reason to?"

"Did I?"

"That's what I'm trying to determine here."

"Well, determine if she had a reason while you're at it, Detective."

Fisher started to tremble, started to blubber, tears trickling down his cheeks. The guy was losing it; spinning out of control and looking for an exit.

"Tell me where you got the cell," said Munroe.

Fisher said, "I got mugged on Monday, my cell was stolen."

Munroe scowled. "Mugged? You didn't say that. Did you report this crime?"

Fisher glared at Munroe. "What would be the point, Detective? Only adds to the workload. Catching criminals gets in the way of paperwork, doesn't it?"

Munroe raised his eyebrow. "We caught you," he said.

"But I'm not a criminal."

"No, sure, the guy who steals a cell: he's the criminal; not the husband who butchers his family. And anyway, cell phone crime's high on the agenda in this precinct. Our chief got his stolen the other day. He was making a call on the station steps. Kid races up and snatches it straight out of his hand – whoosh, gone. So you see, Fisher: you'd have been a priority. My guess is that the chief's got a shoot-to-kill order out on cell phone thieves this week." Munroe scratched his chin and stared at the bagged phone. Eyes on the cell, he said, "Tell me what happened. Entertain me, Mr Fisher."

Fisher sighed. "I was walking to my car. This guy, he whacks me on the head, I fall, I'm confused, he's rifling through my pockets, he takes my cell and races away."

"Anything else? Wallet? Car keys? Copy of Insurance Weekly?"

"My cell, that's all. Maybe he was scared, I don't know. He grabs my cell and he's gone."

"Okay. Then what?"

"Next morning, there's a black guy outside work. He's got a suitcase filled with cell phones. All new, still packaged. He asks if I need a cell and I said I did, so I had a look."

"A guy on the sidewalk with a suitcase."

"I needed a cell. I don't have time to stroll down to the store. I'm working all hours, Detective."

Munroe picked up the bag. "So you buy this one. Yesterday morning."

"Yes. I went home. Didn't set it up. Left it in the kitchen, in my briefcase. Then, this morning ..."

"Yeah, this morning. Ring-a-ding-ding. 'Hey, Paulie, this is The Voice In Your Head speaking – kill your wife, pal; kill your children. Go, Paulie, go. Kill them all, kill them all'. Is that how it happened? You heard a voice on your new cell phone telling you to commit murder?"

Fisher's face was the colour of ash. Dark, heavy bags weighed down his eyes. Streaks of dry tears crisscrossed his cheeks. He's breaking, thought Munroe; coming apart.

Fisher said, "I told you: it was a sequence. Numbers. Five, and then – "

The cell phone rang.

Munroe and Fisher opened their mouths and looked at the phone. It did a little dance in the plastic bag, buzzing like a trapped insect. Munroe and Fisher looked at each other, and Munroe said, "You expecting a call?"

Fisher shook his head slowly and glared at the bag, his face grey and his mouth open.

The phone kept ringing. The screen flashed the words private number at Munroe. He unclipped the bag and slid the pulsing phone out on the desk. The cell hummed and vibrated. "Why didn't you change this damn ring tone?"

"I didn't get around to it."

Munroe picked up the cell phone and said, "They're persistent – whoever they are."

"It was like that this morning. It kept ringing. It was in my briefcase, and it took me a few minutes to dig it out. But it kept on ringing, kept on ringing."

The phone's vibrations sent shudders up Munroe's arm. He guessed this was how construction workers felt when they used those drills to dig up a road. Munroe pressed the answer button and put the phone to his ear and said, "Hello?"

A hiss leached into his head and from the hiss, a voice said, "Seven... Thr..."

He heard a sequence of numbers, but it was only the "seven" he would remember. Munroe felt his memories melt away. They slid off the surface of his mind. He lost himself and became something else.

He pulled a pen from his breast pocket and pushed it into Fisher's eye. The eye popped and spilled liquid. Fisher screeched and fell off his chair.

Munroe stood, the phone pressed to his ear. He tossed the desk aside and stepped towards Fisher. Munroe heard the door crash open behind him and men rushed in. They were shouting but what they shouted was strange to him. He straddled Fisher and tried to drive the pen deeper into his eye.

Men were saying, "Munroe, Munroe," and they dragged him away.

Fisher screamed and scuttled off, blood pumping from his eye. Crown went after him, trying to calm him down, make sure he was okay – however okay a man could be with a pen sticking out of his head.

The phone was still jammed against Munroe's ear and he became aware of the static on the line; of the strong hands gripping his body; of Tommassi saying, "Oh my God, Munroe, oh my God."

Munroe's name and who he was, and his life and his boys, came back to him. He saw where he was and what had happened.

The door burst open. Albeck stormed in. He stood, hands on hips, gun holstered at his waist. Steam billowed from his nostrils. The Chief said, "What the hell have you done, Munroe?"

Munroe started to shake.

Albeck said, "I'm going to–"

A cell phone rang.

Munroe's guts turned liquid.

Albeck furrowed his brow. "That shouldn't happen. It's new, I–" and he dug into his pocket for the phone. The tiny black thing buzzed in his huge wet hand. He looked at it like it was a bug that he could've crushed if he wanted to.

Munroe thrashed against Tommassi and Lewis, saying, "No, no, no, don't – "

Albeck answered the phone.

"This is Alb – "

Munroe kicked and jerked and screamed, no, no, no.

And he saw Albeck's face sag, the colour seep from the skin, the eyes glaze over, the mouth drop open.

Tommassi said, "Chief? You okay? You don't look yourself."

Munroe wailed his sons' names.

Albeck took out his gun.

Lewis said, "Chief, what are you – ?"

Albeck started shooting.

# THE JANTOT HOURGLASS

"IT IS CURSED, YOU know," said the dealer.

"I'm not surprised at that price," said Bellow, looking at the sand timer.

The dealer flapped his hand "But it is rare. The only one of its kind. Jantot's masterpiece."

"Still," said Bellow, flicking the price tag, "that is somewhat obscene."

The dealer shrugged. "It is a remarkable object. Do you collect?"

Bellow breathed. The shop's musty odour filled his nostrils. He looked around. The store was heaped with junk.

Bellow said, "It's for my daughter. A birthday present."

"She appreciates the finer things, does she?"

"It's her hobby, these sand timers."

The dealer clicked his tongue. "I see. Good."

"She has hundreds, but they're trinkets, mostly. I bought her the first one when she was five. It only cost me a pound. She's been fascinated ever since."

In his mind, he watched her grow and mourned what he had missed. He shut his eyes. The guilt rose up. He steeled himself, and it leached away, and in its place came fatigue, pressing against him.

He stifled a yawn and glanced out of the window. The midday sun splintered off the Merc's black shell. Bellow's bodyguards scanned the street.

"Long journey, sir?" said the dealer.

"I flew in this morning. I fly back in – " Bellow checked his watch " – three hours."

"You came to Budapest especially?"

"I came for the Jantot."

"Not many do. We tend not to advertise. We are ... exclusive. Finding us is one thing; but tracing the Jantot to our establishment – that is an achievement indeed." The dealer tilted his head, waiting for an explanation.

Bellow said nothing. He loosened his tie. He looked at the price tag again. Tammy's worth it, he thought. He wanted her to have everything. The guilt of leaving when she was eight, of only having her growing up in his mind, lay heavy in his chest.

The dealer brushed dust from the sand timer. It stood eighteen inches. The four pillars that made up its frame were carved into eight angels. The angels were in pairs, feet to feet. Four of the figures were upright, their arms stretched upwards holding up the top of the hourglass. The other four figures were upside down, arms outstretched to grasp the base of the sand timer. A narrow pipe linked the glass spheres, and the sand inside was golden.

Bellow wanted to see the sand trickle through the tube.

He reached out to turn over the hourglass. The dealer clutched his wrist and said, "Don't you know the story?"

Bellow glared at the man. "Don't touch me," he said, his voice still and cold.

## THOMAS EMSON

The dealer let go of Bellow's wrist. "My apologies."

Bellow let the spurt of anger drizzle away. He glanced at his watch. "How much do you want?"

The dealer held up the tag. "That much."

Bellow fought against a yawn. He took out his chequebook.

The dealer started to pack the hourglass. Bellow watched him and thought of Tammy.

She was wearing a skirt that was too high and a top that was too low when she told Bellow about Jantot's Hourglass. He was taking his daughter to a party in Mayfair. They were sitting in the back of the limo. Music blared from the speakers.

It was incongruous: a teenage girl in her going-out clothes, bobbing her head to 50 Cent, telling her father about a 16th century work of art.

She said, "So, Dad: Louis Jantot was a craftsman, yeah. He made, like, sand timers for ships. And he was having a heavy time."

"Had a sixteen-year-old daughter, did he?"

"Ha, ha. He's got guilt over the St Bartholomew's Day Massacre, you see."

"I see."

"August 24th, 1572."

Bellow smiled. Pride bloomed in his chest. His little girl so knowledgeable. He could see her in ten years' time, hailed as a genius, saluted by peers for her grasp of this subject.

The hip-hop throbbing from the speakers irritated him. But it was Tammy's favourite, and although grating, a sweetness was curled up at its centre because whenever it boomed from a speaker, it meant she was around.

Tammy said, "Catholic mobs went on the rampage and slaughtered thousands of Huguenots, who were French Protestants."

Bellow creased his brow. "Oh, yes."

"There were so many bodies in the rivers that no one would eat fish for, like, absolutely ages."

"Sounds delightful."

"Jantot was Catholic, yeah? He took part in the massacre. Killing and that. But later, he felt really, really guilty."

Bellow glanced out of the window and put a hand over his mouth.

"So guilty that he renounced God. I mean: what kind of God would sanction such brutality, yeah?"

"Same God as always sanctions it."

"So: Jantot renounces God, and as a penance for killing all those poor Huguenots he started to make this hourglass, this sand timer. It would, like, symbolise how brief life was. You know: the sands of time running out and all that. The story goes that Jantot made a pact with The Devil. Lucifer curses the sand timer. Whoever turns it over dies; Satan had first rights on the victim's soul. Jantot was first. He turned the timer upside down; the sand ran out. They say his wife found him. And she went gaga."

"And the timer?"

"Hidden away by the Church. Like all those banned books and dark secrets that would destroy Christianity. Wouldn't it be amazing, Dad, if the Jantot Hourglass was for real?"

Bellow signed the cheque. His eyes felt heavy. The dealer placed the hourglass in a purple box that had "Antik József, Budapest" written on the side in gold letters. He packed the box with tissue paper.

Bellow gave him the cheque. The dealer looked at it and raised his eyebrows: the sum, although known to the man, still had the power to astonish.

On the journey home, Bellow waited for sleep, but it didn't come. He was ill with fatigue when he got back to the house in Kensington. Tammy texted him earlier to say she'd arrived. He'd not seen her in over a month. She'd been in Tuscany with her mother over the school holidays.

The housekeeper was leaving when Bellow walked through the door. He wished her goodnight, and she bowed her farewell. He went into the living room and put the purple box on the coffee table.

"Dad."

He looked up and smiled. She was in her dressing gown. She came to him and Bellow hugged her.

"Happy birthday, princess."

"What is it?" she said, looking at the box.

"You'll need to open it."

Tammy kneeled next to the table. She studied the box. Then she looked up at Bellow, her eyes wide.

Bellow said, "Open it."

Tammy lifted the lid and put it on the table. She looked in the box. She reached inside. Her hands sank into the tissue paper. Her mouth dropped open and she gasped. She lifted her arms, and the Jantot Hourglass rose from the tissue paper. Tammy was shaking. She held up the sand timer and her stare ranged over the piece. Her muscles tensed as the sand timer's weight pulled at her.

"Here," said Bellow, moving the box aside so Tammy could rest the Jantot on the coffee table.

She put it down, her eyes fixed on it, her mouth open.

"It's the Jantot," she said, her voice a whisper.

"Is it all right?"

"Dad, it's more than all right. This is the best present ever."

He sat down. "What did mum get you?"

"A car." She said it as if it were a pair of socks.

He wanted to say, "So this is better?", but instead he said, "That's very kind of her."

"I can't believe it. Where did you get it? How did you find it?"

He told her. Not everything, but most of it: he left out the money he paid those historians and investigators and priests; the priests, most of all.

Bellow's eyes started to close. His body demanded rest. He put his face in his hands.

Tammy said, "Shall I turn it over?"

Bellow hesitated, holding his breath. Then he smiled and said, "Yes, why not."

Tammy turned the hourglass. The sand trickled through the tube.

"I'm going to ring James," she said, jumping to her feet. "I've got to tell him."

Bellow heard her run upstairs. He watched the sand filter through the tube. He stared at the emptying sphere. Tammy's muffled voice drifted from upstairs. She was on the phone to her lay-about boyfriend. Bellow's eyelids drooped. He dropped into darkness.

His eyes snapped open. "Tammy?"

The hourglass stood on the coffee table. The sand had seeped through into the bottom bulb. How long had it taken?

"Tammy?" He got up and listened for her voice, but it wasn't there. The hairs at his nape prickled.

"Tammy?" He stood at the bottom of the stairs. He looked over his shoulder at the Jantot Hourglass. The sand in the bottom sphere pushed up against the sides of the globe and dipped at the centre: it looked like a grin.

Bellow started upstairs. A chill laced his insides. He reached Tammy's bedroom door and he trembled. He knew what he would find.

Bellow opened the door and stood still.

He stared at her for a long time and waited for her to get up off the floor, and for her eyes to blink and her mouth to close, and for blood to redden her grey cheeks. But she didn't get up; and her eyes continued to gaze at nothing, her lips stayed apart, and no blood moved around her body.

He rushed to her and he shook her and said "Tammy" over and over, but Tammy stayed limp and pale and gone.

Bellow said "no, no, no" and tore at his hair and thrashed his head from side to side as grief gouged an endless cavern in his chest.

# **WHERE MOTH AND RUST DESTROY**

MYA DREAMED OF HER zombie father coming down the stairs to eat her.

In her dream she was six. Six like she'd been when the temperatures soared, and the dead came alive to eat the living. Six like she was twenty-one years ago when her mum and a stranger named Sawyer came home just in time to save her from her zombie father.

But in her dream no one came. In her dream Mya's dad attacked and killed her. In her dream she was dead and then her eyes snapped open.

And she woke up.

"Nice nap?" said Zimmer.

She blinked, her eyes adjusting to the bright, brilliant sun.

"Lovely, thanks," she said. "Are we nearly there?"

"Nearly," said Zimmer.

"How far?"

He glanced at the HGV's dashboard. "Another hour, I'd say."

She drank water from the canteen and grimaced.

"You shouldn't leave the canteen out in the heat," she said. "Put it in the ice box, Zimmer."

"You giving me orders, now?"

"I'm just saying."

His face reddened. "I'm driver, you're escort. No way you tell me – "

"Okay, I get it."

Anything for a quiet life, she thought. Anything not to draw attention to herself. But Zimmer wasn't done.

"No way," he said, "you tell me what to do. No idea how you ran things up north, darling, but down here – "

"I get it, Zimmer."

They lapsed into silence. She tried not to think about things too much. She fixed on the grey and empty road. It had once been called the M20. Along its verges lay the rusting hulks of army vehicles. Military Land Rovers and armoured personnel carriers ditched by soldiers. Even the charred wreck of a helicopter. All were remnants of the war against the zombies. A war humans lost.

Zimmer drove past what had once been a tank. It triggered a memory in Mya. Twenty-one years ago, with her mother and Sawyer, Mya had fled a zombie-plagued London. They had driven out of the city and found an abandoned tank in the middle of the motorway. Surrounding it were the remains of soldiers, killed by the undead. Eaten to death. Like most of the population had been eaten to death.

Now as Zimmer drove, Mya scanned the road. A cluster of zombies were gathered up on the ridge. They were squatting over a pile of meat, clawing at it, scooping it into their mouths, their faces red with blood. It was probably human meat. Some poor sod stranded on the highway perhaps, hijacked as he or she made their way somewhere. Two decades after the dead rose, the living were still trying to flee. In this new world of the dead, you were either food, breeder, or worker. You had to be.

But some people tried to escape it. And they ended up like that poor sod on the ridge.

Zimmer said, "You're a pretty thing, it's a wonder you've not been hauled in for the breeding programme."

Her skin crawled. "I'm infertile."

"Right. They didn't just make you food, then? That's what they normally do, ain't it. If you ain't got a skill, I mean. If you ain't no use to them. At least you're of a use as food."

"Well, I've got a skill."

"Oh yeah."

"Yeah, Zimmer – I'm willing to die for my fellow humans." She smiled at him. He gawped, losing control of the truck for a second. The HGV swerved across the motorway. "Careful, Zimmer," she said. "I never said I'd die for you, mate."

"Hey, that's a joke ain't it? Yeah? You're joking. What you said, what you said there, that's what those Human First fellas say. You ain't one of them nutters? You ain't... "

"No, Zimmer, chill out."

"You sure?"

"Yeah, sure," she said.

"So... so what skill you got?"

"I'm a mechanic. Why do you think I was assigned to you?"

"Who knows? Far as I'm concerned, you're just an escort. This needs two people, this lark. I'd never do it solo, never. You ever been to a Z-World?"

Mya shook her head. "Be first time today."

"Treat for you, doll."

"Not your doll, Zimmer."

"Being friendly. What's wrong in calling you 'doll'? You don't remember the time before the dead, do you?"

"A little. I was six when it happened."

"Political correctness everywhere – you couldn't say boo to a goose, let alone call it a goose. Had to call it, I don't know, feathered sentient being, or something. Bollocks, it was. And women," he glanced at her, "you wanted to be like men, you did."

"You made sure we didn't after the dead, though," said Mya.

"What do you mean?"

"Crimes against women increased in those early days after the plague. Rape was – "

Zimmer shuffled in his seat and said, "Yeah, whatever."

She thought for a second, her gaze scanning the empty motorway as they drove north. And then she said, "Sometimes I think it was for the best the zombies took control."

"True enough," said Zimmer.

"Slavery agrees with us humans, don't you think?"

"Well… keeps us on the straight and narrow. You step out of line, you're food. Simple, really."

After a few minutes silence Zimmer spoke again.

"You know," he said, "before all this happened, I was a Christian."

"You were?"

"Yeah, a real Fundie-type. Creationist, you know? God made the world in six days and all that crap."

"Some people will believe anything."

"And evolution, well, I suppose I never understood it, but there was no way I believed in it – till the zombies showed me it was real."

"It's real."

"I mean, they changed so quickly. Every generation different. And now, look at 'em – they're running the country."

"Kind of."

"What d'you mean?"

"Zimmer, it's anarchy. Human society has collapsed. We're either food, breeders, or... or people like us, workers."

"Least we're alive."

"I wouldn't call it living."

He glared at her. "You do sound like those Human First folk, girl. Are you sure you're not – "

"I need a pee."

"You what?"

"Pee, I need to pee."

"We're only half-an-hour away, can't you hold?"

"No, I can't."

Zimmer grumbled. He stopped the HGV in the middle of the carriageway. You could do that these days. At least the problem of congestion had been solved in the years after the dead.

"Thanks, Zimmer. Hey, you want a drink?"

"You what?"

"A drink. While you're waiting."

"A drink? What do you mean a drink?"

"You know what I mean."

"You serious?"

"I am serious."

"Where... where d'you get booze?"

"Oh, you know. Plenty of moonshine around."

"They'll kill you if they find out. Makes the flesh taste bad. Pickles it and they hate that."

"They were never worried at the beginning. They'd eat anything."

"Bit more choosy these days," said Zimmer. "So where is it?"

Mya leaned over the seat and retrieved her ruck sack. Out of it she pulled a dark brown bottle. Zimmer eyed it eagerly, licking his lips.

"What is it?" he said.

"I don't know? Booze. Just booze. You want it?"

Zimmer nodded, and she gave him the bottle. As she stepped down from the cab, her heartbeat quickened, and a cold sweat soaked her back.

She clambered up the slope at the side of the road, not looking back to see if Zimmer was drinking or not.

She went over the ridge and scooted down the other side on her backside. She sat on the grass, in the warm summer sun, and stared out over the remains of Maidstone. The city looked dead. Mya shivered, knowing its streets crawled with zombies. The inner-city dead. Thousands of them still living on instinct as opposed to intelligence.

Most of the evolved zombies now inhabited the Z-World centres. Hundreds of them lived permanently at the resorts, while many more gathered there for the great feedings in December and June. Zimmer and Mya were going to the facility based at the former London Zoo in Regent's Park. It was the June feeding. It would be the first time Mya would witness the event. It would also be the last. She cried a little, mourning the things that would die that night.

She closed her eyes for a moment and said words that resembled a prayer, but she didn't know who she was praying to.

She went back to the truck and found Zimmer slumped across the seat. She climbed into the cab and nudged him, saying his name. He snorted. Mya took a deep breath and got out of the cab again. She walked round to the rear of the truck, listening to the noises coming from inside the trailer. She tried not to listen.

She looked up the road. It was empty, clear, barren.

From her pocket she took a signalling device. It was the size of a key fob. She pressed the red button. A green light on the gadget blinked.

Mya sat on the side of the road.

Twenty minutes later a lorry appeared on the horizon, shimmering in the heat.

Mya got to her feet and waited for the vehicle. As it came nearer, she saw that it towed a trailer. It was the same as the one she and Zimmer were taking to London. The same apart from its cargo.

She waited, and the truck came.

Three men leapt out and one came to Mya and they kissed, his hand gently resting on her stomach.

Then they went to work.

After what had to be done was done, the men and the truck left. Mya watched and pined for the man who had kissed her and touched her belly. She sighed and turned and went back to the cab to see if Zimmer had recovered.

She was about to nudge him awake when she spotted the manifest lying on the seat next to him. Mya picked up the clipboard and read the sheet of paper in the plastic sleeve. The words chilled her.

*Delivery 472B/3*
*Dover to Z-World, Regent's Park*
*200 bred humans – A-Category/Norfolk*

*Aged: 12-40*

"A-Category" meant the highest quality meat. Organically reared humans. Well maintained livestock cultivated in the countryside. Not the factory-bred flesh delivered to the inner cities where the zombie population had surged, and the less-evolved undead had settled. As the manifest noted, this batch had come from Norfolk. It had been delivered to Dover the previous day. Now it was on its way to London to be eaten.

Mya shook off the horror and poked the driver in the arm.

"Zimmer," she said, "Zimmer, wake up."

He jerked and mumbled something. Spit dribbled down his chin. His breath smelled of booze. He came to, blinking and scrabbling around.

"You all right, Zimmer?"

"How... how long've I been... asleep?"

"Not long," she said.

He sat up and groaned, holding his head. The sleeping pills Mya had powdered into the beer the previous night made Zimmer woozy, and they would give him a headache.

"Never felt so bad after booze," he said. "What the hell was that stuff?"

He kicked the bottle away. Mya picked it up and tossed it outside. It smashed on the road. Beer spilled. She smelled it and then shut the door.

"You want me to drive, Zimmer?"

"You can't drive."

"You want to bet?"

"I'm the driver."

"Get going, then."

"Christ," he said and started the truck. "My head feels like someone's drumming inside it. Can't believe I – shit, oh shit."

"What now?"

"Is that the time?"

"Probably."

"We're late, we're badly late."

Mya said nothing. She appeared cool, not bothered they were late for their appointment. Inside she trembled with fear. Part of her was relieved the trailer had been swapped, while another was terrified she'd be found out before getting to Z-World. The cargo trucks were always in danger of zombie attacks. They would be the less developed kind, mostly originals from the first days of the plague. They were brutal and mindless. They were relentless, and in days nearly wiped out the human population.

The country became known as Zombie Britannica.

Zombies do not reproduce through sex. They reproduce through death. Death gives birth to them. Their victims are resurrected, as is anyone who dies from natural causes.

As more zombies were made, mutations occurred in their genes. Some mutations produced intelligence.

As the undead regenerated, a few populations showed more brainpower than their predecessors.

Ten years ago, the first zombies with language abilities appeared. These were basic grunts, a few words, simple sentences.

But as the decade wore on, those communication skills grew more complex. The zombies evolved. They learned to think. They learned to control their nature. As a result, they became deadlier than ever. They became nearly human.

"Do I smell of booze?" said Zimmer. "Because if I do, they... they'll... Jesus, I'm dead."

"Here," said Mya, offering him a mint from a paper bag.

"You're a right black marketeer, ain't you. Booze, mints... what else can you get us?"

She said nothing.

He glanced at her and said, "Well, you a black marketeer or not?"

"'Course I'm not. I got the booze off a mate, he's a moonshiner up in the borders. I bought the sweets at the market in Dover yesterday."

Dover. Hell on earth. A town that used to have a population of just under 30,000 now groaned under the weight of nearly 150,000. When the plague struck, thousands went there, hoping to cross to the Continent. But the ferries stopped sailing. There was no escape. And no one knew if the Continent was safe. Most of the people who came to Dover, stayed. And then more came. And more. Buildings were ransacked. Battles broke out between locals and incomers. There was no law to control the outbreaks of violence. Zombie attacks also caused panic and fear. But gradually, a fragile peace settled over the town.

It became what it was now – an enormous refugee camp.

Similar camps were found across Britain, mostly in the port towns – Portsmouth, Holyhead, Liverpool, Felixstowe, Hull, Leith, Aberdeen.

As the zombies evolved, they saw value in these over-populated, disease-ridden slums. They saw a food supply.

And in recent years, the zombie leadership realized that without humans, they would die out.

It was another development that made them more human – the ability to recognise their own mortality.

In the months after the dead came alive, the surviving humans formed small communities. Over the years, as the zombies evolved, they took advantage of this anthropological development. They appointed human leaders in these communities. Militias roamed the camps, maintaining order. The people despised the leaders and the militia because they were collaborators, working with the new breed of zombies.

But the work continued.

Warehouses were commandeered to store humans selected for food. They were usually troublemakers, or anyone the camp leaders disliked. Prisons housed breeding programmes. The healthier and genetically-blessed humans were kennelled at these sites to produce the next generation. Stock was selected from these programmes and sent to rural areas. These humans were housed in villages and small towns. They were reared organically as food for the zombies residing at a Z-World resort.

Every human was potentially food, but you could save yourself by either becoming a worker – you had to be fit and strong – or a breeder – you had to be attractive and healthy.

Mya and Zimmer had been handed their duties the previous night – a cargo of food for Z-World in London.

While she was listening to the foreman handing out the orders, Mya could hear the whimpers and cries of the humans in the trailer.

She tried to ignore them, just as she'd been taught to. But it was difficult. Her instinct was to open the trailer and tell those poor, doomed people to run.

Had she done that, she would have been zombie meat.

Best to wait. Best to stick to the plan.

And that's what she was doing as they drove along Primrose Hill near Regent's Park. This road used to be called leafy. Now it was overgrown, the hedges and trees unkempt and uncared for. The road was rutted, and rusted vehicles lined the way.

Overhead, crows circled. Mya shuddered. The birds were there for food – and the way they croaked and wheeled suggested there was already meat waiting for them down below.

"Almost there," said Zimmer. "Now listen up, girl. Since you never been to one of these Z-World places before, there are things to remember, right?"

"I'm listening," she said.

---

Fifteen minutes later, after Zimmer's lecture, they arrived at the entrance to the old London Zoo. The sign depicting animals remained, but it was now red with blood, and the words Z-World had been painted roughly across it.

Two figures armed with shotguns and wearing fluorescent bibs guarded the gate.

Zimmer rolled down his window and said, "Morning," to the guard on his side.

Mya looked out of her window. The second guard looked up at her. Half his face was gone. His bony hands grasped the shotgun. He grinned at Mya. Saliva oozed from his mouth.

Zombies with guns, she thought. What could be worse?

She looked away.

By that time, the first guard had checked Zimmer's manifest and waved them through the gates.

"Welcome to Z-World, London," Zimmer said. "Where zombies come to sunbathe and to slaughter."

Mya was shivering. Her fear grew. She was in hell, now – really in enemy territory. If she put a foot wrong, the zombies would kill her. No questions asked. No mercy given.

Zimmer drove the truck slowly along the road. On each side were cages and enclosures once used to house animals. Now people were stored in the pens and paddocks.

Mya thought her heart would burst when she saw a group of children, aged around nine or ten, reaching through the bars of a cage. Their little faces were creased with horror and tears stained their cheeks. For a moment Mya couldn't breathe, panic clutching at her chest. But as Zimmer drove by, and the children went past, she mastered her horror again. She had to keep herself together.

Zombies watched Mya and Zimmer as they drove. They had stopped to stare at the truck. They knew it contained food, their feast for the June feeding.

"Told you," said Zimmer, "don't look 'em in the eye – they'll take it as a challenge and might just go for us."

Hundreds of zombies were strolling along the paths that snaked around the resort. They moved in groups or individually. There didn't seem to be much interaction between them. Some leaned over to look down at the humans in the enclosures. The undead snarled and growled at the terrified people.

Mya's chest flared with rage.

She wanted to kill every zombie here. If she had a gun, she might just have leapt out of the cab and started firing, blowing the heads off those monsters.

But she wouldn't last long. She was one against many. Zombies cared little about their kind. So what if some died? As long as they got to you, that was all that mattered.

During the war, waves of zombies charged the army. The undead were mown down in their hundreds. But behind the first wave more came. More and more and more. The dead sea was unstoppable. Military action failed. Humanity was defeated.

"Here we are," said Zimmer.

He stopped the truck in front of some single-storey buildings. There was a swimming pool to the right. It contained no water, just bones and litter. Next to the pool a female zombie lounged on a sun-bed. She wore bikini bottoms. She had no need of the top because her breasts were gone. The whole front of her body was gone, and Mya could see into the cavity. The woman sat up and brushed her long, grey hair out of her face, and then curled back her lips and dribbled.

Mya followed Zimmer out of the cab. The heat was stifling. The smell of decay hung in the air. A rich, ripe odour that made Mya retch.

"Your companion feeling somewhat under the weather, Zimmer?" said a voice.

Mya turned towards it. Approaching them was a figure dressed in a black fedora and a long black coat. Sunglasses hid his eyes. His face was chalk-white. The skin on his hands was peeled to show bones and ligaments.

"I am Geller, I run this facility," said the black-clad. "Who are you?"

"Her name's Asher, Mr Geller," said Zimmer.

"Mya Asher," said Mya.

"Asher, I see. New to duties, are you? What skill keeps you from being food at my table?"

"I'm a mechanic," she said.

"Plenty of those around," said the zombie. "Well, you are late, Zimmer."

Zimmer rubbed his hands together. "We... we had some trouble with the truck, Mr Geller."

"That's why you have a mechanic."

"Yes," said Zimmer, "and she... she sorted things out."

Geller grunted. He was dribbling a little. Mya knew that was probably because he was near humans.

We're his food, thought Mya. His instinct is to eat us, and he wants to eat us right now – but he's evolved the ability to control his nature.

She trembled with nerves and looked around.

The woman by the pool had lain down again.

"How many zombies here this summer?" said Mya.

"This summer?" said Geller. "We have three-hundred and twenty guests, seventy-eight residents. Why do you ask?"

"Interested. I've never been to a Z-World before."

"No? How did you not end up as food, Asher?" asked the zombie.

She looked him straight in the face. "I worked on the docks up in Leith. I was on a ground team, repairing trucks that ferried cargo to Scottish Z-Worlds."

"And you came south?"

"My family was from this area. Before the... "

"I see," said Geller. He looked her up and down. "You could have been on the breeding programme. You appear fit, healthy – genetically-blessed."

"She's barren," said Zimmer.

Mya quaked but held Geller's stare. Her mouth was dry, and she was terrified that she'd be found out.

The zombie said, "Take the truck into the vehicle bay, leave it there till tonight. Your quarters have been prepared."

Zimmer and Mya turned to go back to the HGV, but Geller called after them, "Wait a minute."

Mya turned, dread chewing at her belly.

Geller said, "You didn't come across a crew of Human First scum on your journey, did you?"

Mya could feel the blood leaching out of her brain, and it made her giddy.

"We didn't see anyone," said Zimmer and then turned to Mya. "You see anyone when I had a nap?"

Eyes on Geller she said, "There was no one."

He said, "Found them on the road, coming from your direction. They had stolen cargo on them."

"Stolen?" said Zimmer. "Who from?"

"We don't know. You've not let the consignment out of your sight the whole journey, have you, Zimmer?"

"Absolutely not, Mr Geller."

"I would have the trailer opened to check – "

Mya stiffened.

Zimmer said, "But that would – "

"I know, I know," said Geller. "It would damage the stock, let some fresh air in." He licked his lips. Spit oozed from his mouth. "Humans are better when they're ripe. A nice odour of decay on the meat. And it makes it softer. Too much exposure to fresh air spoils that a little. Always best to keep them in that humid condition provided so well by your trucks, eh? What do you say, Asher?"

"I say... " Mya's mouth was dry. "I say, of course."

"Of course," said Geller. "Follow me. I'll show you."

Geller led them behind the buildings and towards an enclosure. Zombies were leaning over the wall, snarling at something down below. Mya's skin goose fleshed. Her fear mounted.

"Here we are," said Geller as they reached the wall.

Mya had to use all the military training she'd received at the Human First camps in the north of Scotland to stop herself from screaming.

Down in the enclosure, three men had been tied to trees. The men were naked and they were screaming. Their bodies were covered in wounds. Blood soaked the ground. Chunks of meat torn out of their bodies were strewn around.

Mya wanted to leap over the wall and go to the men, to one in particular – the one who had kissed her and laid a hand on her belly.

But she controlled her emotions. It was difficult. Inside she was wailing.

Geller lifted his hand. A door opened at the back of the enclosure.

A huge zombie burst out of the entrance. The giant was naked and had enormous muscles. Its flesh was grey, and parts of its scalp were missing, showing the skull underneath.

It was a 'roid zombie. One of the monsters this new, evolved zombie society had pumped full of growth hormone for their own entertainment.

The 'roid zombies were used in gladiatorial-style games, where they were pitted against the best of humanity – former professional fighters, soldiers, hard men.

There was only ever one winner in those contests.

Humans were no longer the alpha species.

The monster charged at the men tied to the trees. They shrieked. The zombie tore a chunk from one man's thigh. The victim howled in pain.

Mya stared in horror as the zombie grabbed the man in the centre – her man. The creature sank its teeth into her lover's arm. He cried out and caught Mya's eye. Seeing her intensified his terror, and she saw this. She wheeled away just as the zombie bit through her lover's arm, and all she heard as she staggered away was his squeals of anguish.

---

An hour later in their quarters, Zimmer said, "Why d'you run off like that?"

"We didn't need to see that."

"You know what they're like."

"I do know what they're like."

"They're just scaring us, that's all."

"They do that anyway. There's no need for… "

"What?" said Zimmer.

She was shaking, tears in her eyes.

"You knew those men," said Zimmer.

Mya rubbed her eyes with a towel. "Of course not."

"You did, Mya. You knew them. You're Human First."

She looked at him. He was sitting on his bunk. The cabin was bare apart from the two beds. A door on the back wall led to a toilet and washbasin. They would stay here till after the feeding, then, in the early hours of the morning, drive back to Dover.

Zimmer shook his head. "Don't believe it."

"What don't you believe?"

"You're arrogant, you lot."

"Arrogant?" she said.

"We're trying to get along, trying to stay alive, and you... you lot just spoil everything – you put the rest of us in danger. You're not Human First, you're Me First, Us First. Sod the rest of humanity."

"How old are you, Zimmer?"

"Fifty."

"Getting on, now."

"I'm all right."

"There'll be younger drivers wanting your job, soon. Younger, fitter."

"So?"

"What do you think happens to you when you're surplus to requirements?"

He said nothing.

Mya said, "You'll end up as food, that's what. And being you're overweight, older, bad skin, you'll be shipped to the inner cities. Tossed out in the streets with a bunch of other oldies where you'll be hunted down by first-born zombies. The originals. The ones you can't talk to, Zimmer. You can't beg and reason with them, you know that. They'll rip you apart. You're food. That's what we all are. Is that what you think you deserve?"

"I... I just want to live."

"You won't. You'll die in agony like those men out there today. You'll be eaten alive. No questions. You know that. It's how we all go. It's human destiny – to be devoured."

"Christ," he said, putting his head in his hands.

"We're at least trying to do something, trying to maintain human dignity," said Mya.

He looked at her. "Tell me what you're doing here?"

She told him.

"Christ," he said. "You failed, then?"

"Failed?"

"The cargo we were carrying, the cargo your friends stole, it's ended up here anyway. Those people are going to get eaten. You failed."

"No... no, we didn't." And she told him why.

After they talked, Zimmer agreed to go with her to where the truck had been parked.

It was night. Howls and screams filled the air. Torches burned, lighting the resort. Humans cried and begged.

At midnight, the great feeding would begin. The human cargo would be released into the grounds of Z-World. Two hundred men, women, and children. Add to that the hundreds already caged at the old zoo, it would mean that nearly a thousand humans would be stampeding through the resort.

And then the zombies would hunt them. Nearly four hundred monsters unleashed.

The zombies would savage the humans. They would eat them. Kill them all. The screams of the dying would echo across London. Z-World would be swimming in blood and gore. Death would be everywhere. There would be no human survivors.

"Are you wearing your badge?" said Zimmer.

"Yes," Mya said, indicating the red, cotton square pinned to her jacket. It marked a human worker out from food. The identification was vital if you were delivering to a Z-World. Any human wandering around without the marker would either be killed on the spot or thrown into an enclosure or cage for eating later.

Zimmer and Mya stayed in the shadows and made their way to the vehicle bays.

"I can't believe you drugged me and swapped this trailer," said Zimmer, standing near the container that stored his original cargo.

Mya could hear the humans whimper inside.

"You put me in danger," he said. "I'm still waiting for an apology."

"I'll not say sorry for trying to save the human race."

"At the cost of human lives?"

"People die in wars. It's sad, but it happens. How many will die and suffer if we don't do anything?"

"Maybe I won't. That's all that matters to me."

She said nothing.

"You're not infertile are you," said Zimmer.

She looked him in the eye.

"In fact," he said, "you're pregnant."

"How do you know?"

"Just guessed. The way you were rubbing your belly when we were watching those poor buggers in the enclosure, the way – "

"One of them is the father – was the father."

"And you're going to sacrifice your baby for a victory you may never achieve? Is that what you're saying?"

"It's... it's for the future. I have a younger sister. She was born soon after the plague. She's six years younger than me. She's pregnant, too, and I want her children to have a world worth living in."

"What about your child?"

"It's ... it's the price we pay for freedom."

"What did the dad think?"

"He understood."

"Now he's dead, and you'll be dead too."

Mya went over to Zimmer's truck and squatted next to the trailer her lover and his two companions had attached to it hours earlier.

She was reaching under the trailer, feeling for something. Something that had been taped there so she could use it in an emergency.

"What are you looking for?" said Zimmer.

"For a – " She found it and froze.

Two figures came from the shadows, one of them a giant.

"Busy, are we?" said Geller, still wearing his hat and sunglasses. Behind him the 'roid zombie snarled. Its teeth had been filed into points. Mya imagined them ripping through her lover's flesh.

"Just... just checking the cargo," said Zimmer.

"You should've done that at 5pm," said Geller.

"Thought we'd check to see where this came from," said Zimmer, banging on the side of the trailer they'd originally towed from Dover.

"Can you tell?" said Geller.

"Might be able to," said Zimmer.

Then Geller looked at Mya. "What are you doing there, Asher?"

Mya jerked at the gun and the tape tore away. She leapt to her feet and trained the weapon on Geller.

He said, "Oh, I see what you're doing."

The 'roid zombie growled and moved forward.

Mya shuffled nervously.

"You're Human First scum, aren't you," said Geller. "Both of you."

"Not me," said Zimmer. "I know nothing about – "

"Shut up," said Geller. "Asher, put down the gun. There's no escape."

"Then you're dead, too," she said.

"I'm already dead," said Geller.

"Well I'll kill you again," said Mya. "You know I can."

Geller smiled. "There's nothing you can do, Asher. Why do you fight? Your world is gone. It's our world now."

"We're taking it back."

"No you're not," said Geller. "Do you know why? You are too weak. You value things too much. You kept gold and money and antiques and art and cars, you stored these things. And did they save you? Jesus warned you, didn't he."

"I don't believe in Jesus."

"You wouldn't," said the black-clad zombie. "That's why you ignored his warning: 'Do not store up for yourselves treasures on earth, where moth and rust destroy.' But you did. And what for? Your money and cars are meaningless. Put the gun away, Asher. Give it up. Accept your fate."

"You're dying, Geller," said Mya. "All of you. Tonight. Z-Worlds across the country are being hit."

"Hit?" he said.

"We're blowing you away."

Geller snarled. "I am going to eat you, legs first. Make my way up your body, slowly. I'll make it hurt so – "

She shot him in the face. His sunglasses shattered. The hat flew off his head. His skull erupted in brain and blood and he hit the ground.

The 'roid zombie charged. Zimmer legged it. Mya, panicking, started firing. Bullets pummelled the monster's face, turning it into a bloody maw.

Mya kept firing but she'd emptied the clip.

The 'roid zombie stumbled towards her.

She backed away.

The monster was on her.

She cowered, screaming.

A gunshot made her ears ring.

She smelled cordite.

The ground shook when the 'roid zombie fell, smoke rising from where his head had been.

Mya looked up.

Zimmer was leaning out of his cab with a shotgun jammed into his shoulder. Smoke plumed from the double-barrel.

They looked at each other for a second and Zimmer must have read Mya's thoughts.

"I keep it for insurance," he said.

Mya nodded.

Zimmer said, "You get going, they'll be here any second."

"You what?" she said.

"Get in your boyfriend's truck and take those people out of here, take them anywhere."

"Zimmer, you can't – "

"Just do it. You're right. This is my last drive, they've told me. I tried not to think about it, but it's over. I'm food. You've got your baby, now. Go, Mya, get out of here."

"No," she said, "I've got to set off the explosives."

In the distance, a siren blared. Shouts and screams filled the air.

Zimmer asked, "Where's the detonator?"

Mya gawped.

Zimmer said, "Where is it?"

"Under the trailer's rear wheels," she answered.

"How... how do you... you know ... "

"You... you just open the cover and press the red button. You've got 60 seconds."

"Jesus, plenty of time for them to rip me to pieces."

"Zimmer, you don't have to do this, you – "

"Go, Mya. Just go. Time I did something for the human race. I did nothing before all this happened. Nothing when I thought I was good, when I went to church. Go. Get in that other truck, now. I'll give you a minute, then I'm detonating. How much explosives in that trailer?"

"Enough to make a crater out of Regent's Park."

He nodded. "Go, now."

As she drove along the roads of Z-World, running over zombies as she went, tears streamed down her face.

She hoped Zimmer would have enough time.

She hoped he would not suffer.

She hoped.

Armed zombies fired at her, but they caused little damage. 'Roid zombies tried to stand in her way, but she drove over them.

She put her foot down, the big truck roaring down the road, past the cages full of children, towards the zoo's entrance.

Mya felt sick. All these humans would die. But she couldn't save them all. She would save two hundred, those in her trailer. That would be something. She wept, hating herself for letting those people in the cages and the enclosures die. But as her lover said, this was war. She'd been ready to die herself. Sacrifice was necessary. And at least the poor sods wouldn't be eaten alive. Death would be very quick for them.

She smashed through the gates and hit the Outer Circle road.

Behind her, the sky lit up. An orange glow filled the darkness. And seconds later, an explosion deafened her and the lorry bucked.

Mya screamed as the trailer swung out behind her. For a moment, she thought she'd lose control of the HGV. But she managed to keep from tipping over. She accelerated.

If she failed to get far enough from the blast, the people in the trailer would be baked alive.

She felt the heat from the explosion now. The earth trembled. A dark cloud of debris and smoke suddenly started to spread from the epicentre of the blast.

It was catching her up, rolling down the road behind her like a wave.

But Mya kept driving. She had lives to save. Two hundred in the trailer, and one in her womb.

She drove without looking back.

Finally, as she left London, she slowed down and glanced in her side-mirrors. A great fire raged in the centre of the city, lighting up the night. The cloud of dust had covered Central London and was seeping into the outskirts now.

An hour later on the M1, 70 miles outside London at the Watford Gap Service Area, Mya stopped and opened the trailer.

The smell was terrible. Humans staggered out, crying and screaming. They were sweaty and dirty, covered in their own shit and blood. As they poured out, Mya noticed that some were dead. Dozens of them. They would have to be burned or soon they would rise as zombies.

"Where do we go?" said a man, his bright blue eyes standing out against his dirty face.

"I... I don't know," she said.

"Where are you going?"

"North. Scotland."

"Are... are you Human First?"

She nodded.

"Take us," said the man.

"How?"

"In the trailer. We've been in it for twenty-four hours waiting for death. I think we can bear it for a few hours more if we know we're going to live."

The crowd had gathered behind him. They murmured in agreement: "Take us, take us."

Mya thought for a second.

Then she said, "Take your dead out and burn them. There should be some fuel in the petrol station in the service area."

"Burn them?" said the man.

"Burn them," she said.

"But... you're Human First, you don't – "

"They're not human anymore," said Mya. "Do it. And keep watch. I'm going to have some shut eye in the cab."

Mya fell asleep to the smell of burning flesh, and she dreamed of her unborn child, a daughter, she was sure, waiting for her nine months in the future.

# ABOUT THE AUTHOR

THOMAS EMSON has written eight horror novels, all published by Snowbooks. Among his books are the werewolf novel Maneater; vampire thriller Skarlet and its sequels; and the Jack the Ripper novel, Pariah. He has also published a non-fiction book called How To Write A Novel In 6 Months. His novels have been translated into Italian and Turkish. For more information visit the author's Twitter feed @thomasemson or his website thomasemson.com. For rights, please contact Thomas's agent Mariam Keen at the Whispering Buffalo Literary Agency.

# ALSO BY THOMAS EMSON

**available at amazon**

## HOW TO WRITE A NOVEL IN 6 MONTHS

A published author's guide to writing a 50,000-word book in 24 weeks

**THOMAS EMSON**

★★★★★
There's no "bull" here, nor is it an ego trip, nor a flyer for further sales, he just shares the method that has worked for him
—Biro man

★★★★★
My bookshelves are groaning with books on how to write but this is by far the best yet —Gail C.

★★★★★
Easy to follow, well written with real life experience. A must for all budding writer
—Gary Cousin

★★★★★
Its honesty and matter-of-fact tone, combined with a "doable" strategy, has given me boost I needed
—D. Barley

★★★★★
Provided me with the tools and confidence to embark on my debut novel
—Jason Minick

★★★★★
Thomas Emson makes you feel like you are capable of anything and doesn't over complicate it —Shanric

★★★★★
Having followed Mr Emson's guide, I have finally published a novel on Amazon
—Steve J. Jones

# Acknowledgments

THANK you as always to my wife, the memoirist and ghostwriter, Marnie Summerfield Smith, whose support is constant and unwavering. Gratitude to my agent Mariam Keen, who looks out for me. I also appreciate the eagle eye of Holly Kirwan-Newman, who has read these stories for me, and is a very fine proof-reader indeed. A special thank-you to all my readers, without whose backing I really wouldn't write.

*Thomas Emson, 2019*